It's Fine
to Be Nine

It's Fine to Be Nine

A
LITTLE APPLE
PAPERBACK

SCHOLASTIC INC.
New York Toronto London Auckland Sydney

From TALES OF A FOURTH GRADE NOTHING by Judy Blume, illustrated by Roy Doty. Text copyright © 1972 by Judy Blume, illustrations copyright © 1972 by E. P. Dutton & Co. Used by permission of Dutton's Children's Books, a division of Penguin Putnam Inc.

From THE CHALK BOX KID by Clyde Robert Bulla, illustrated by Thomas B. Allen. Text copyright © 1987 by Clyde Robert Bulla. Illustrations copyright © 1987 by Thomas B. Allen. Reprinted by permission of Random House, Inc.

Text, pp. 76–93, three illustrations from RAMONA FOREVER, by Beverly Cleary. Illustrated by Alan Tiegreen. Copyright © 1984 by Beverly Cleary. By permission of Morrow Junior Books, a division of William Morrow & Company, Inc.

From FOURTH-GRADERS DON'T BELIEVE IN WITCHES by Terri Fields. Copyright © 1989 by Terri Fields. Reprinted by permission of Scholastic Inc.

Text, pp. 73–82 ("The Gathering of David Bernsteins") with one illustration, from THE ADVENTURES OF ALI BABA BERNSTEIN by Johanna Hurwitz. Illustrated by Gail Owens. Text copyright © 1985 by Johanna Hurwitz. Illustrations copyright © 1985 by Gail Owens. By permission of Morrow Junior Books, a division of William Morrow & Company, Inc.

From PIPPI LONGSTOCKING by Astrid Lindgren, translated by Florence Lamborn. Translation copyright © 1950 by the Viking Press, Inc., renewed © 1978 by Viking Penguin Inc. Used by permission of Viking Penguin, a division of Penguin Putnam Inc.

From SKYLARK by Patricia MacLachlan. Copyright © 1994 by Patricia MacLachlan. Used by permission of HarperCollins Publishers.

From FOURTH GRADE IS A JINX by Colleen O'Shaughnessy McKenna. Copyright © 1989 by Colleen O'Shaughnessy McKenna. Reprinted by permission of Scholastic Inc.

BEING NINE IS JUST FINE by Patricia C. McKissack. Copyright © 1998 by Patricia C. McKissack.

Reprinted with the permission of Simon & Schuster Books for Young Readers, an imprint of Simon & Schuster Children's Publishing Division, from THE HOBOKEN CHICKEN EMERGENCY by D. Manus Pinkwater. Copyright © 1977 by D. Manus Pinkwater.

From THE FLUNKING OF JOSHUA T. BATES by Susan Shreve, illustrated by Diane de Groat. Text copyright © 1984 by Susan Shreve. Illustrations copyright © 1984 by Diane de Groat. Reprinted by permission of Alfred A. Knopf, Inc.

From FOURTH GRADE RATS by Jerry Spinelli. Copyright © 1991 by Jerry Spinelli. Reprinted by permission of Scholastic Inc.

ISBN 0-590-38604-2

Compilation copyright © 1998 by Scholastic Inc.
All rights reserved. Published by Scholastic Inc.
LITTLE APPLE PAPERBACKS, SCHOLASTIC and associated logos are trademarks and/or registered trademarks of Scholastic Inc.

12 11 10 9 8 7 6 5 4 3 2   8 9/9 0 1 2 3/0

Printed in the U.S.A.   40

First Scholastic printing, September 1998

Contents

Introduction   vii

1. From *Tales of a Fourth Grade Nothing*
   by Judy Blume   1

2. From *The Chalk Box Kid*
   by Clyde Robert Bulla   10

3. From *Ramona Forever*
   by Beverly Cleary   21

4. From *Fourth-Graders Don't Believe
   in Witches* by Terri Fields   36

5. From *The Adventures of Ali Baba
   Bernstein* by Johanna Hurwitz   50

6. From *Pippi Longstocking*
   by Astrid Lindgren   59

7. From *Skylark*
   by Patricia MacLachlan   72

8. From *Fourth Grade Is a Jinx*
   by Colleen O'Shaughnessy McKenna   81

9. *Being Nine Is Just Fine*
   by Patricia C. McKissack   92

10. From *The Hoboken Chicken
    Emergency* by Daniel Pinkwater   105

11. From *The Flunking of
    Joshua T. Bates* by Susan Shreve   116

12. From *Fourth Grade Rats*
    by Jerry Spinelli   125

Introduction

It isn't always easy to be nine. Ramona Quimby sure knows that. She's having all kinds of new experiences when she learns that she'll no longer be the baby of the family when the *new* baby, whom the Quimbys have named "It" for now, comes.

Peter Hatcher knows the feeling. His troublemaking little brother, Fudge, is always stealing all the attention. Sound familiar? Ramona and Peter are young readers' favorite characters from Beverly Cleary's *Ramona Forever* and Judy Blume's *Tales of a Fourth Grade Nothing*.

In this collection of stories excerpted from books by some of the greatest, award-winning writers for young people, you'll meet kids who wish they were older and kids who wish they were younger. Kids who have problems with their brothers and sisters and kids who have problems at school. Stories about best friends and worst enemies. In other words — life. There's even a story about a boy with a 266-pound chicken!

"Forget it, dude. You can't go backwards. Time marches on." That's what Suds's friend

Joey tells him in Jerry Spinelli's *Fourth Grade Rats* when Suds wishes he could go back to third grade. Joshua T. Bates, the character in *The Flunking of Joshua T. Bates*, wishes he was *anywhere* but back in third grade when he finds out he has to repeat it.

What could all these characters possibly have in common? They're all nine years old, and their lives are funny and sometimes hard, and even, in the case of a girl named Pippi Longstocking, downright weird. Collected here are twelve stories to remind you: It's fine to be nine!

It's Fine to Be Nine

From
Tales of a Fourth Grade Nothing
by Judy Blume

9

*One of Judy Blume's most beloved characters,
Peter Hatcher, has a big problem, and its name
is Fudge. Peter's baby brother, Fudge, is always
causing trouble, like the time he lost their father's big account, Juicy-O, by covering the
client's suitcases with stickers. He's always
taking Peter's pet turtle, Dribble, without permission and throwing temper tantrums. Most
of all, with a cute baby like Fudge around, no
one pays much attention to Peter.*

Nobody ever came right out and said that
Fudge was the reason my father lost the
Juicy-O account. But I thought about it. My
father said he was glad to be rid of Mr. Yarby.
Now he could spend more time on his other
clients — like the Toddle-Bike company. My
father is in charge of their new TV commercial.

I thought maybe he could use me in it
since I know how to stand on my head. But

1

he said he wasn't planning on having any head-standers in the commercial.

I learned to stand on my head in gym class. I'm pretty good at it too. I can stay up for as long as three minutes. I showed my mother, my father, and Fudge how I can do it right in the living room. They were all impressed. Especially Fudge. He wanted to do it too. So I turned him upside down and tried to teach him. But he always tumbled over backwards.

Right after I learned to stand on my head Fudge stopped eating. He did it suddenly. One day he ate fine and the next day nothing. "No eat!" he told my mother.

She didn't pay too much attention to him until the third day. When he still refused to eat she got upset. "You've got to eat, Fudgie," she said. "You want to grow up to be big and strong, don't you?"

"No grow!" Fudge said.

That night my mother told my father how worried she was about Fudge. So my father did tricks for him while my mother stood over his chair trying to get some food into his mouth. But nothing worked. Not even juggling oranges.

Finally my mother got the brilliant idea of me standing on my head while she fed Fudge.

I wasn't very excited about standing on my head in the kitchen. The floor is awfully hard in there. But my mother begged me. She said, "It's very important for Fudge to eat. Please help us, Peter."

So I stood on my head. When Fudge saw me upside down he clapped his hands and laughed. When he laughs he opens his mouth. That's when my mother stuffed some baked potato into it.

But the next morning I put my foot down. "No! I don't want to stand on my head in the kitchen. Or anywhere else!" I added. "And if I don't hurry I'll be late for school."

"Don't you care if your brother starves?"

"No!" I told her.

"Peter! What an awful thing to say."

"Oh . . . he'll eat when he gets hungry. Why don't you just leave him alone!"

That afternoon when I came home from school I found my brother on the kitchen floor playing with boxes of cereals and raisins and dried apricots. My mother was begging him to eat.

"No, no, no!" Fudge shouted. He made a terrible mess, dumping everything on the floor.

"Please stand on your head, Peter," my mother said. "It's the only way he'll eat."

3

"No!" I told her. "I'm not going to stand on my head anymore." I went into my room and slammed the door. I played with Dribble until suppertime. Nobody ever worries about me the way they worry about Fudge. If I decided not to eat they'd probably never even notice!

That night during dinner Fudge hid under the kitchen table. He said, "I'm a doggie. Woof . . . woof . . . woof!"

It was hard to eat with him under the table pulling on my legs. I waited for my father to say something. But he didn't.

Finally my mother jumped up. "I know," she said. "If Fudgie's a doggie he wants to eat on the floor! Right?"

If you ask me Fudge never even thought about that. But he liked the idea a lot. He barked and nodded his head. So my mother fixed his plate and put it under the table. Then she reached down and petted him, like he was a real dog.

My father said, "Aren't we carrying this a little too far?"

My mother didn't answer.

Fudge ate two bites of his dinner.

My mother was satisfied.

After a week of having him eat under the table I felt like we really did have a family

4

dog. I thought how great it would be if we could trade in Fudge for a nice cocker spaniel. That would solve all my problems. I'd walk him and feed him and play with him. He could even sleep on the edge of my bed at night. But of course that was wishful thinking. My brother is here to stay. And there's nothing much I can do about it.

Grandma came over with a million ideas about getting Fudge to eat. She tricked him by making milk shakes in a blender. When Fudge wasn't looking she threw in an egg. Then she told him if he drank it all up there would be a surprise in the bottom of the glass. The first time he believed her. He finished his milk shake. But all he saw was an empty glass. There wasn't any surprise! Fudge got so mad he threw the glass down. It smashed into little pieces. After that Grandma left.

The next day my mother dragged Fudge to Dr. Cone's office. He told her to leave him alone. That Fudge would eat when he got hungry.

I reminded my mother that I'd told her the same thing — and for free! But I guess my mother didn't believe either one of us because she took Fudge to see three more doctors. None of them could find a thing wrong with my brother. One doctor even suggested that my mother cook Fudge his favorite foods.

So that night my mother broiled lamb chops just for Fudge. The rest of us ate stew. She served him the two lamb chops on his plate under the table. Just the smell of them was enough to make my stomach growl. I thought it was mean of my mother to make them for Fudge and not for me.

Fudge looked at his lamb chops for a few minutes. Then he pushed his plate away. "No!" he said. "No chops!"

"Fudgie . . . you'll starve!" my mother cried. "You *must* eat!"

"No chops! Corn Flakes," Fudge said. "Want Corn Flakes!"

My mother ran to get the cereal for Fudge. "You can eat the chops if you want them, Peter," she told me.

I reached down and helped myself to the lamb chops. My mother handed Fudge his bowl of cereal. But he didn't eat it. He sat at my feet and looked up at me. He watched me eat his chops.

"Eat your cereal!" my father said.

"NO! NO EAT CEREAL!" Fudge yelled.

My father was really mad. His face turned

bright red. He said, "Fudge, you will eat that cereal or you will wear it!"

This was turning out to be fun after all, I thought. And the lamb chops were really tasty. I dipped the bone in some Ketchup and chewed away.

Fudge messed around with his cereal for a minute. Then he looked at my father and said, "NO EAT . . . NO EAT . . . NO EAT!"

My father wiped his mouth with his napkin, pushed back his chair, and got up from the table. He picked up the bowl of cereal in one hand, and Fudge in the other. He carried them both into the bathroom. I went along, nibbling on a bone, to see what was going to happen.

My father stood Fudge in the tub and dumped the whole bowl of cereal right over his head. Fudge screamed. He sure can scream loud.

My father motioned for me to go back to the kitchen. He joined us in a minute. We sat down and finished our dinner. Fudge kept on screaming. My mother wanted to go to him but my father told her to stay where she was. He'd had enough of Fudge's monkey business at meal times.

I think my mother was relieved that my fa-

ther had taken over. For once my brother got what he deserved. And I was glad!

The next day Fudge sat at the table again. In his little red booster chair, where he belongs. He ate everything my mother put in front of him. "No more doggie," he told us.

And for a long time after that his favorite expression was "eat it or wear it!"

From
The Chalk Box Kid
by Clyde Robert Bulla

Gregory is a good artist. He even has a nick-name, the Paintbrush Kid, but since he moved to a new school he hasn't felt much like paint-ing. When he discovers a burned-out building that used to be a chalk factory, he decides to turn it into a garden. In his garden he can grow anything he wants, but what will the kids at school think when they find out the truth about his garden?

When Gregory got home from school, he went straight to his garden. He was thinking about the fountain. The garden spread over three walls. He would have to take out some-thing to make room for the fountain. But he liked to change things.

He started to the garage to get the ladder. He stopped. There were footsteps outside the gate. Someone laughed. Someone went "Shh!"

The gate opened. Boys and girls came pushing in. They were all from Room 3.

Vance was the leader. He said, "We came to see your garden."

"Where is it?" asked one of the girls.

"*This* is it," said Vance.

"It's just a burned-out building," said someone else.

"Didn't I tell you?" said Vance. "It's nothing. It's nothing at all."

He turned and walked out. The others followed him. And the last one out was Ivy!

She looked back. She almost stopped. Then she was gone.

That night Gregory wasn't hungry. There was chocolate chip ice cream for dessert. It was his favorite, but he couldn't eat it.

Mother felt his forehead. "It feels hot. I think you should be in bed."

He went to bed. She sat with him.

"Gregory, what's wrong?" she asked.

He began to tell her. "Some of the others at school have gardens. I said I had one too."

"Why did you say that?" she asked.

"Because I do have one," he said. "It isn't like theirs, but it's a garden."

"The one you made in the burned building?" she asked.

11

"Yes. And after school they followed me home. They came in to look, and they said —"

"What did they say?"

"They said it was nothing at all. They thought I was just bragging."

"And you weren't bragging?"

"No. I wasn't. Maybe I was pretending — a little — but I wasn't bragging. They can think what they want to," he said. "I don't care!"

*   *   *

But it was hard for him to go to school the next day. When he got there, he walked around the block before he went in. He was the last one in Room 3.

Miss Perry smiled at him. He didn't think she knew. But the others did. He could feel them looking at him.

Ivy sat up front. Miss Perry spoke to her. "Are you going to make us a picture today?"

Ivy had brought her leather case to school. She didn't answer Miss Perry. She stood up and came straight to Gregory. She put the case down on his desk and went back to her seat.

The room was still.

Miss Perry looked puzzled. She asked, "Do you want Gregory to use your paints and brushes?"

"They're not mine," said Ivy.

"Of course they are," said Miss Perry.

"No," said Ivy. "They're Gregory's."

"How could they be Gregory's?" asked Miss Perry.

"Because — because his pictures are better than mine," said Ivy. "I saw them on the walls. And they're better!"

Miss Perry looked more puzzled than ever. "What walls? Gregory, do you know what she means?"

He told her, "She means the walls in back of my house. I made a garden there — out of chalk."

"Out of *chalk*?" said Miss Perry.

"That's my garden," he said. "That's the one I talked about."

"I see." Miss Perry came back and picked up the leather case. "This is yours, Ivy," she said. "It's part of your prize, and your name is on it. But if Gregory's pictures are as good as you say, I can see why you want him to have a prize too." She put the case down on Ivy's desk.

The bell rang. School began.

At noon Miss Perry said to Gregory, "I'd like to see these walls of yours. And I'm sure Miss Cartright would too. When may we see them?"

"Anytime," he said.

"Today after school?" she asked.

"Yes," he said.

They walked home with him after school, Miss Perry and Miss Cartright. He opened the gate for them.

Miss Perry said, "Oh!"

Miss Cartright said, "It really *is* a garden!"

They looked at the walls and talked to each other. They sounded excited.

"The pictures he did in art were nice, but nothing like this!" said Miss Cartright. "I heard him say a piece of paper wasn't big enough. I think he needed a whole wall!"

Miss Perry asked him, "Where did you get the idea for this?"

"From Mr. Hiller," he said.

"I want him to see it," said Miss Perry.

Mr. Hiller came to see the garden.

"I'd like a picture of this," he said. "A big

picture to put up in the nursery. May I bring my camera over tomorrow?"

"Yes," said Gregory.

On the way out Mr. Hiller met Daddy. Daddy had just come home from work.

"Are you this boy's father?" asked Mr. Hiller.

"I am," said Daddy.

"I just saw Gregory's garden," said Mr. Hiller. "You must be proud."

"Proud?" said Daddy.

"Yes, proud," said Mr. Hiller, and he left.

Mother came out. "Who was that?"

"I don't know," said Daddy, "but I think we'd better see what is behind our house."

They went out into the burned building. Gregory went with them.

Mother looked at the walls. "Oh, Gregory!"

"We'll have to get new clothes," said Daddy.

"New clothes?" asked Mother.

"Yes," said Daddy, "because our son is going to be famous and everybody will be looking at us."

Mother called Uncle Max, and he came out. He looked at the garden for a while. "First he was the Paintbrush Kid," he said. "Now he's the Chalk Box Kid."

It sounded like a joke, but Uncle Max wasn't laughing. And that night, when Gre-

gory went to bed, he saw his old pictures on the wall.

"Where are your posters?" he asked his uncle.

"I took them down," said Uncle Max.

Things were different at school. Everyone he met was friendly. Even Vance was friendly. "There's a picture of your garden down at the nursery," he said. "Why don't you go see it?"

But the best thing of all happened one evening after school. Gregory was making a place for his fountain when Ivy came to the gate and looked it. A little boy was with her.

"This is my brother Richard," she said. "I brought him to see."

Gregory had piled up bricks and made places to sit. The three of them sat on the bricks in front of the walls.

Ivy whispered to her brother, "This isn't like our garden, Richard. This is different. This is somebody else's garden."

"I see it," said the little boy.

Gregory told Ivy, "I'm putting in a fountain. Do you want to help me?"

"I don't know," she whispered. "I might."

Then they were quiet, and they sat there for a long time.

From
Ramona Forever
by Beverly Cleary

9

The story of Ramona continues, and there are many changes in the Quimby household. They are expecting a new addition to the family and Ramona's father is about to finish college and become a teacher. Ramona worries about no longer being the baby in the family. She's not sure she's ready to be the middle child.

Now that the news of the baby was out, Beezus and Ramona had no more trouble getting along with one another after school. Saying they were sorry and burying Picky-picky had brought them closer together. Their parents said nothing more about their returning to the Kemps' after school.

Ramona began to feel that life was humdrum. Even the weather was dreary — wet and cold, but not cold enough to snow. She tried wearing a Chiquita banana sticker plastered to her forehead when she went to school,

to start a fad like the sticker fad in Aunt
Beatrice's third grade. Her aunt said she
sometimes felt as if she were teaching a
bunch of bananas. Members of Ramona's
class said, "What are you wearing that for?"
or "That looks dumb."

Then Ramona tried announcing, "We're
going to have a new baby at our house."
No one was interested. New babies were
common in the families of her classmates.
Because she had been to their homes, Ramona knew what new babies meant — a
stroller in the hall, a playpen in the living
room, a high chair in the kitchen, tiny clothes
strewn around, plastic toys underfoot, zwie-

back crumbs sticking to chairs. Of course she could not expect her friends to get excited about the Quimbys' new baby.

Weeks went by. Aunt Beatrice telephoned almost every evening to ask how her sister was feeling. The conversation of the grown-up sisters was filled with laughter, which puzzled Ramona and Beezus, who failed to see why having a baby was funny. They hung around, trying to guess what the laughter was about from their mother's side of the mysterious conversations. They were able to guess that Aunt Bea was very busy, that she went skiing almost every weekend, but the ski season would soon be over. Their mother's remarks were meaningless. "Why, Bea!" "I don't believe it!" "What did Michael say?" "No. No, I won't tell the girls."

Both Beezus and Ramona pounced on their mother when a conversation ended. "What won't you tell us?" they demanded.

"If I told you, you would know," answered their mother.

"Mother-*er*!" protested Ramona. "You're just plain mean."

"Yes, exasperating," agreed Beezus.

"Me?" Mrs. Quimby looked innocent. "Mean? Exasperating? Wherever did you get that idea?"

23

"Did Michael ask Aunt Bea to marry him?" demanded Beezus, eager for romance.

"Not that I know of," answered their provoking mother.

Ramona stamped her foot. "Mother, you stop it! You're getting to be as bad as Howie's Uncle Hobart, always teasing."

"Heaven forbid that I should be like Howie's Uncle Hobart," answered Mrs. Quimby, still teasing. "I'll have to try to mend my ways."

Ramona was strict with her mother. "See that you do," she said. "I don't like mysteries, except in books."

Mr. Quimby, who was trying to study at the dining room table, frowned during all these conversations that disturbed his work. Something dreadful called a midterm was about to happen at the University. He was worried and nervous. The girls could tell because he made more jokes than usual. When he was worried, he always joked. When he saw Ramona lying on the floor looking at TV, he said, "There's Ramona. Batteries not included."

However, Mr. Quimby's studies would be over the middle of June, when he would receive his teaching credential a few weeks before the baby, known as It, was due. Then he would work during the summer as a checker at one of the Shop-rite markets to replace checkers who took vacations. By September, he would have found a place in a school, if not in Portland, at least in a suburb. Mrs. Quimby would leave her job to take care of It, which pleased Ramona. The house always seemed so empty without her mother.

Of course, Beezus and Ramona were eager to know if It would be a boy or girl. Ramona wanted a boy. Beezus wanted a girl. Their parents said they would take whatever came along.

The girls were concerned with other questions. Whose room would It share? How long would their mother stay home to take care of It? Ramona wanted her mother home for keeps — babies weren't much work, they just lay around all day. Maybe her mother could find time to let down the hems of Ramona's skirts and pants and bake a few cookies. Beezus wished she could stay home from school to take care of It herself. However, she had the summer to look forward to. Mrs. Quimby said that after the girls' father found a job and It was a few months old, she would like to take some evening courses at the University. "And I'll take care of It while you study," said Beezus.

"Enough of It," said Mr. Quimby. "No

child of ours is going to be called It Quimby. Think of how everyone would laugh when the teacher called the roll. How would you feel introducing your new brother or sister by saying, 'This is It'? And every time anyone said, 'I don't like it,' about bread pudding or stupid TV programs, It's feelings would be hurt."

The family agreed that of course the baby needed a real name. Robert Quimby, Junior? Maybe, if It turned out to be a boy. Mrs. Quimby said the baby would not be named after herself because she had never liked being called Dorothy. Ramona thought Aston Martin would be good for a boy. She had heard the name someplace and thought it sounded nice. Beezus preferred Gary or Burt for a boy and thought April was a pretty name for a girl, except It would be born in July, which was not a name for a person.

Then Mr. Quimby brought home a pamphlet from the drugstore, called *A Name for Your Baby*, which listed names and their meanings. Ramona immediately found her own name and discovered that Ramona meant "wise helper." How boring, she thought, and hoped this did not mean that she would be expected to change It's diapers or anything like that.

Beezus, on the other hand, laughed when she discovered Beatrice meant "heavenly one." "Whee!" she said, twirling around the living room and flapping her arms like wings. Her complexion had improved, which made her happier about everything.

Together the girls studied the pamphlet. Many names would not do at all. Philbert, which meant "superior," sounded good with Quimby, but at school, boys would call him a nut. Beezus thought Abelard might be a good name for a boy because it meant "romantic hero," but Ramona pointed out that everyone at school would call him "Lard." Beezus also thought Lorelei, which meant "romantic siren," was a pretty name for a girl until Ramona began to chant, "Loreliar, Loreliar, pants on fire."

Ramona preferred Gwendolyn for a girl because the name meant "fair." If she had to have another sister, she wanted one who always played fair.

Mr. Quimby suggested names that were much too fancy — Alphonso Horatio, Clarinda Hepzibah, or Quentin Quincy Quimby. His daughters, however, did not take him seriously. This was more of his joking because he was worried.

"What if It is twins?" Ramona's thought

presented a whole new problem. She studied the pamphlet once more. Paul and Pauline? Boris and Doris? Gerald and Geraldine?

"They could be two girls or two boys," Beezus pointed out.

"Abby and Gabby," said Mr. Quimby. "Peter and Mosquiter."

"Daddy, you're just being silly." Ramona was always stern with her father when she felt he had gone too far with his jokes.

Mrs. Quimby asked what was wrong with plain names like Jane or John. Nothing, agreed her daughters, but fancy names were more fun to look up. They discovered that Hobart meant "clever," but of course they weren't going to name their baby after Howie's uncle.

Finally It came to be known as Algie. When Mrs. Quimby could no longer squeeze into her clothes and changed to maternity clothes, Mr. Quimby recited:

> *"Algie went out walking.*
> *Algie met a bear.*
> *The bear was bulgy.*
> *The bulge was Algie."*

Mrs. Quimby said, "You wouldn't think it was so funny if men had babies." However, she laughed and referred to the new baby as Algie after that. The girls, when told that Algie was short for Algernon, looked up the name and discovered it meant "courageous."

"Of course, we couldn't really name it Algernon," said practical Beezus. "Everyone at school would make fun of him. Nobody is named Algernon except in old-fashioned books."

Besides the fun of finding names, Beezus and Mrs. Quimby watched for sales of baby clothes. Ramona's diapers, inherited from Beezus, had long ago been used for dust cloths, much to Ramona's relief. She did not like to be reminded that she had ever worn diapers. "On TV, babies wear disposable diapers," she told her mother.

"Much too expensive," said Mrs. Quimby.

All the Quimbys' needs seemed too expensive. Still no letters arrived asking Mr. Quimby to report for an interview. "Maybe I should go to Saudi Arabia like Old Moneybags, work double shifts, and earn enough to pay off our bills and the mortgage, and buy a car that wouldn't eat us out of house and home in repair bills," he said thoughtfully. This time his daughters were sure he was joking.

"Bob, please be practical," said Mrs. Quimby. "You have no engineering experience." Because she needed exercise, she left for her evening walk.

Ramona decided to go along because she wanted to talk privately to her mother. As they walked beneath the budding trees, she began by saying, "When Algie comes, I won't be your baby anymore."

"That's right," agreed her mother. "You will be my middle child, with a special place right in the middle of my heart. And when Algie comes, I will be home, so we can spend more time together. Daddy will have found a teaching job by then."

Ramona was comforted. They walked in silence for a while before she asked another question that had been worrying her. "Does Algie hurt you?"

Mrs. Quimby's smile was reassuring. "No, he doesn't hurt me, but he does kick." She laid Ramona's hand on the bulge that was Algie, and sure enough, Ramona felt a kick so tiny it was almost a flutter. Ramona was stunned by the miracle of that little kick and was silent all the way home.

Mr. Quimby began to work double shifts weekends at the frozen-food warehouse. He looked so tired and discouraged that his daughters were frightened. Somewhere, some-place, there must be a school that wanted

their father. Nothing in the world was worse than unhappy parents. Nothing. When parents were unhappy, the whole world seemed to go wrong. The weather even seemed rainier, although this was probably in Beezus's and Ramona's imaginations. Their part of Oregon was noted for rain.

Then one day a letter did arrive, offering Mr. Quimby a teaching position in a one-room schoolhouse, grades one through eight, in a town no one had ever heard of, in southeastern Oregon. Beezus ran out to the car for the road map. "That's *miles* away," she said when she had searched the map and found the town. "It's miles from anyplace. It isn't even on a red line on the map. It's on a black and white line, almost in Idaho."

"What's in that part of the country?" wondered Mrs. Quimby who, along with her husband, had lived in Oregon all her life but never visited that corner of the state.

"Sagebrush, I guess." Mr. Quimby was vague. "Juniper, lava rocks. I don't know."

"Sheep. I learned that in school." Beezus did not seem happy about her knowledge.

"Hooray for the Portland public schools." Mr. Quimby's hooray did not express excitement.

"Lambs are cute," ventured Ramona, hoping to make her father feel better about his offer.

"But our house," said Mrs. Quimby, "and a new baby." No one had thought that the family might have to move.

"And Picky-picky's grave." Ramona assumed her most sorrowful expression. "We would have to leave his little grave."

"If I were single," Mr. Quimby seemed to be thinking out loud, "I might enjoy teaching in a one-room schoolhouse for a year or two."

But you've got us, thought Ramona, and I don't want to leave Howie and my friends at school and Aunt Bea and all our nice neighbors.

"It sounds like Laura Ingalls Wilder," said Beezus, "only with sheep."

"Bob —" Mrs. Quimby hesitated. "If you want to take the job, we could rent our house. A small town might be an interesting experience for the girls until you found a job in the city."

Strangers in their house, some bratty child in her room, marking up her walls with crayons. Please, Daddy, thought Ramona with clenched fists, please, please say no.

Mr. Quimby sat tapping the end of a ball-point pen against his teeth. His family waited, each thinking of the changes that might be made in her life. "No freeways," he said, as if he were still thinking out loud. "Blue skies, wide open spaces."

"We have blue skies here," said Ramona. "Except when it rains."

"No big library," said Beezus. "Maybe no library at all."

Mrs. Quimby kissed her husband on the forehead. "Why don't we think it over a few days? Now that you've had one offer, another might come along."

"Good idea," announced Mr. Quimby, "but I need a steady income, and soon." He patted the bulge that was Algie.

"Daddy," ventured Ramona, "if you don't teach in that school, promise you won't leave us and go to that Arabian Nights place. Please."

"Not with Algie on the way." Mr. Quimby hugged Ramona. "Anyway, I understand that camels spit."

"Just like Howie's Uncle Hobart used to do," said Ramona.

Somehow the whole family felt better knowing that one school wanted Mr. Quimby, even if he was not sure he wanted the school.

From
Fourth-Graders Don't Believe in Witches
by Terri Fields

9

When strange things start happening at Allan's new neighbor's house, he begins to suspect that she is a witch. But he's not scared away. In fact, he's determined to find out the truth!

I should never have told my mother that I hated coming home to an empty house after school. I only said it because of Bobby Alexander. He'd tried almost the exact same words on his mom, and the next week she had quit her job and even volunteered to be his Cub Scout den leader.

I thought that sounded pretty nice. Besides, I didn't exactly love being a latchkey kid. I was always afraid I'd lose my key or something, and sometimes, I just wished I had someone to tell about my day. Since Mom hadn't been working for all that long, I figured she might not mind quitting if someone like me gave her a good reason why she should.

My plan seemed so simple that I still have trouble figuring out how it got so botched up. Things started off well enough. As soon as my mom got home from work, I put on my saddest-looking face and waited for her to ask me what was wrong. I had to hold that look for a long time, since she took her time coming in and putting away her coat. But finally she sat down next to me and asked about my day. When she did, I looked extra upset and said, "I just hate being here all by myself every day after school. Maybe, if you quit work . . ."

At first, Mom got a very worried look on her face. "But Allan, I have to work . . ." She walked back and forth across the room, almost talking to herself. "I just can't be home, but maybe you really shouldn't be here all alone, especially if it's upsetting you."

Mom happened to glance out the window as she paced. Suddenly she exclaimed, "Why, that's it! Why didn't I think of it before! I'll bet that nice older lady who moved into the Millers' old house would be glad to take care of you!"

"But Mom," I protested. This was not the way things were supposed to be happening. "I don't want a baby-sitter." She didn't stop to listen; instead, she headed out the door and down the street. I watched her knock on the door of the old cottage two houses down. Oh, no, I thought as the door opened and my mother went inside.

She stayed there a long time. I kept my fingers crossed, hoping it was because the lady was explaining that she didn't want to baby-sit. After all, we didn't even know her; she'd only moved in a couple of weeks ago. I kept looking out the window, wishing Mom would hurry home and make it official that I was still on my own. I mean, I didn't want some old lady taking care of me; I wanted my mom home.

Finally Mom walked back into our house. "Well, that's settled," she said with a pleased grin on her face. "Actually I haven't been very happy about your being home alone, either." She went into the kitchen to start dinner, and I followed her explaining that I really didn't need some old-lady baby-sitter at our house. "Oh, Allan. She's not some old-lady baby-sitter. Her name is Mrs. Mullins, and she seems quite nice. You'll like her. She prefers that you go to her house, which should be a rather fun adventure, don't you think?"

I didn't think it would be a fun adventure at all; in fact, I was sure I would hate it, but Mom didn't wait for my answer. She just added, "Mrs. Mullins will be expecting you every day after school starting tomorrow, and you can stay there until I get home."

Mom was so pleased that she began to hum while she made dinner, but I groaned loudly. There were lots of latchkey kids in my class, and none of them had baby-sitters. When everyone found out about my baby-sitter, the kids would tease me forever. I wasn't exactly Mr. Popularity now, and I sure didn't need it going around the school that I was a baby. With that awful thought in mind, I even gave up my favorite TV program to spend every minute I could until bedtime trying to talk my mother out of this baby-sitter idea. "I was only kidding about being lonely," I said. I begged, I argued, I even told her that if I were home alone, I would clean up the house after school. Mom wouldn't listen. She thought the whole idea of my going to Mrs. Mullins's was terrific, and nothing I said was making any difference at all. That is why I, Allan Hobart, was probably going to be the only kid in the entire fourth grade who was stuck with a baby-sitter. I was mortified.

The next afternoon I walked home from school as slowly as possible, trying to get to Mrs. Mullins's as late as I could. That way I wouldn't have to talk much to her. I knew all about old ladies from the time I'd visited my great-aunt in Maine. They pinched your cheeks, they treated you as if you were two years old, and you had to shout to make them hear anything you said.

Facing all that every day was more than any nine-year-old boy should have to handle. Somehow, I was going to get out of this mess, but about the only way I could think of was to be so terrible that Mrs. Mullins would tell my mother she didn't want me there anymore. I would probably get in a lot of trouble, but it would be better than this.

Stupid Bobby Alexander and his dumb ideas! I thought as I turned up the walkway to Mrs. Mullins's front door. It wasn't fair that his mom was home helping him work on Wolf Pack badges while I was stuck with some awful old lady. Even her house was old. The green paint was peeling off the front door, and the white house showed patches of brown. It had been empty forever. Though we'd never actually done it, my friends and I had talked about trying to sneak in and use it for a clubhouse. Actually it was Jeff, Jason, and Bobby who talked about sneaking in. I was just sort of hanging around them.

Anyway, I never found out whether I could actually go with them or not because before they set a time to sneak in, the For Sale sign went down. I'd crossed my fingers and hoped a family with a nice kid my age would move in. I figured I could get to know him before he knew anyone else, and we might be best friends. Instead, some old lady with no kids at all moved in. Pounding my toe into the sidewalk, I sighed. Then I dragged my feet up the front walk and pushed the doorbell. Mrs. Mullins was probably going to gush about what a cute little boy I was. Ugh! She might even want to read me some fairy tales! I was *not* listening to any fairy tales! Suddenly I realized that no one had answered the door. Maybe she's not here, I hoped. I rang the bell again. If no one answered this time, I could go home, and my mom would be mad at the old lady instead of me. I smiled at the thought.

Just then the door opened. I gulped. It was just as I had suspected. The lady standing there even looked like my great-aunt in Maine. I tried to prepare my cheeks to be pinched, but surprisingly, Mrs. Mullins didn't reach for them. "Oh, it's you," she said sounding annoyed. "Well, I guess you should come in. What's your name again?"

This reception wasn't exactly the gushing excitement I thought it would be, but that was fine. It would probably just make my plan work more easily, and Mrs. Mullins would be glad to get rid of me. Scowling, I shouted loudly to make sure she heard, "My name's Allan, Allan Hobart."

"Well, there's no need to shout about it, and there's certainly no point to standing here letting bugs in. You may enter; shut the door behind you, please."

I scowled even harder in case Mrs. Mullins didn't see too well, because she hadn't mentioned that I looked unhappy. Just in case she wasn't going to notice at all, I said, "I really don't want to be here!"

Mrs. Mullins looked at me and returned my scowl. "Well, that's fine, because I really don't want you to be here, either."

"You don't?" I said, beginning to get confused. "But my mom —"

"Your mother seems very nice, but she certainly is determined. Oh, I tried, I really did. But I couldn't talk her out of the idea that your coming here after school was a wonderful idea. Besides, mothers always get so upset if I try to explain about . . ." Mrs. Mullins's penetrating green eyes grew large and she clamped her mouth firmly shut as if she'd said too much already.

"Explain about what?" I asked.

Mrs. Mullins stared at me the same way my math teacher did when she wasn't sure I'd done my homework. "Never you mind," she sniffed.

There was something about the way she said it that made me sure I wanted to know what it was. "Gee, I won't tell anyone else, really I won't."

"Tell what?" she asked.

"What you started to tell me."

Mrs. Mullins fixed her green eyes on me. "I don't remember starting to tell you anything at all." And with that she turned and walked out of the room.

I stood in the entryway totally confused. This was just great; why did these things always happen to me? Not only was I going to be the laughingstock of the fourth grade for having a baby-sitter, but I had to have the crabbiest one in the whole world. "What a witch!" I said aloud, kicking my foot against the carpet.

With that Mrs. Mullins came bursting back into the room. She put her hands on her hips. "What did you just say?" she demanded.

"Uh, nothing."

Her voice got real high and she said, "Oh, yes, you did. I heard you! What did you say?"

If she heard me, I didn't know why she

needed me to repeat it. I did know that if she told my mom, I'd be in big trouble. I could hear my mom now: "You called that sweet, little lady a witch? Allan Hobart, I'm ashamed. . . ."

Maybe Mrs. Mullins hadn't heard exactly what I'd said. Then again, maybe she had, and if I lied, I'd get in trouble for being rude *and* for lying. It was definitely a no-win situation, so I just didn't say anything.

Mrs. Mullins tapped her foot. "Did you call me a witch?" So she had heard, after all.

I bit my lip. "Well, yeah, but I didn't mean to. What I mean is that . . . uh . . . of course, you're not a witch." I could feel my face getting red.

Mrs. Mullins took a step toward me. "I take it you don't like witches."

This had to be the weirdest lady I'd ever met. How could my mother have done this to me! Mrs. Mullins was waiting for me to say something. "Uh, no, why would anyone like a witch? They're ugly."

"Oh, really?" She seemed interested.

"Yeah, real ugly. And they do terrible things." I was getting warmed up now, and I let my imagination go. It was better than standing in all that silence. "They take bats' wings, and dried-up blood, and old toads, and lots of other gross stuff, and they wait until midnight, and then they make awful spells."

Mrs. Mullins bit her lip, and I thought maybe I'd scared her, which made me feel real bad. "Listen, it's okay, though. You don't have to worry or be scared or anything, because the good news is that there *are* no real witches."

"You know that for certain, do you?"

"Oh, yeah, I'm absolutely sure!" I replied, feeling pretty important. Imagine, me knowing more than an old lady like her. "So you don't have to worry about any dumb witches at all. They can't hurt you because they're just make-believe."

The corners of Mrs. Mullins's mouth began to turn upward, and her eyes started to twinkle. "I see," she replied. Suddenly my blue Cubs baseball cap sailed off my head and began to fly around the room faster and faster. My eyes were getting dizzy following it. Then my hat dropped *kerplop!* at my feet.

"Wow! Did you just see that?" I shouted. "How did that happen?"

Mrs. Mullins didn't say a word. She just turned on her heel and marched out of the room.

I bent over to retrieve my cap and stared

at it very carefully. It was definitely the same Cubs cap that had been on my head only a minute ago. "Hats don't fly," I said to an empty room; yet that was exactly what this hat had just done.

Okay, so it did fly, but there's got to be a reason, I told myself, holding on to it tightly. I thought it over. It's got to be some kind of a trick. I squinted my eyes to see if there was some sort of string on the ceiling, but nothing was there. This was some trick!

Then I thought about Jeff Wilson. He was the most popular kid in the fourth grade; the captain of every team, while I was just the "yeah, I'll take him" kid who never got picked first or last — a nobody to fill up the middle. But suppose, I thought to myself, suppose I could walk in and make everyone's hat fly off his or her head. Then they'd notice! I grinned. This Mrs. Mullins definitely needed more investigation. Anxious to unravel her tricks, I marched into the kitchen.

Mrs. Mullins was sitting at the kitchen table. She had her hand on her chin and her forehead was wrinkled in thought. I waited a minute, not wanting to interrupt her, but it didn't seem as if she was ever going to stop muttering and look at me. "Um, excuse me,"

I said, "but that was a pretty neat trick, I mean with my cap. How did you do it, anyway?"

Mrs. Mullins looked confused. "Trick . . . that wasn't a trick. Look, Allan, I really think it was a mistake for me to say I'd baby-sit. It just isn't going to work out."

"Yes, it will, Mrs. Mullins. Listen, you don't even have to baby-sit me all year or anything. Just teach me how to make hats fly off people's heads."

"I will do no such thing!" She stared at me. "Now, please, just go into the other room and leave me alone."

I'd been totally dismissed. Mrs. Mullins wasn't going to reveal anything, so I walked into what looked like a normal little-old-lady living room and sat down on a blue-flowered sofa. This afternoon sure hadn't been anything like what I'd thought it would be. I decided I'd start looking for the string or wire that must have pulled my cap off my head. First, I walked around the room very slowly, waving my hands in front of me so I'd feel the string. When I found nothing, I crawled around on the floor trying to find a clue to her trick.

Mrs. Mullins entered the room just as I

was lying on my stomach reaching under the sofa. "What are you doing?" she asked. "Are you stuck?"

I jumped up. "I'm fine," I said.

"Oh?" she replied. "Most people sit *on* sofas, not *under* them!" Her green eyes stared at me. I grew more uncomfortable by the minute. Maybe I'd better try talking about something else besides my hat. If I led up to it slowly, maybe she'd tell me how it had flown.

"So, uh, have you been a baby-sitter" (how I hated that word!) "for a lot of kids?"

Mrs. Mullins pushed her wire-rimmed glasses up on her nose. "Not really. Actually you're my first one. And you don't look much like a baby."

I was glad she'd at least noticed. Though I didn't mean to say anything, I blurted out, "You know, you're pretty weird. I mean, haven't all old ladies done lots of baby-sitting?"

She began to tap her foot quickly against the carpet as she folded her arms against her chest. "Well, I've had many other important things to do. I guess I should have been firmer with your mother. I really have no idea what to do with a nine-year-old boy."

This was my opportunity to get out of having Mrs. Mullins as my baby-sitter. I was pretty sure I could get Mrs. Mullins to tell my mom that she didn't want to baby-sit me, but I had a strange feeling I'd be sorry if I did. Mrs. Mullins wasn't like any person I'd ever met. For one thing, old ladies were supposed to think kids like me were just adorable; this one thought I was nothing but a pain in the neck. For another thing, even if I managed to ditch Mrs. Mullins, my mom would only find another baby-sitter, and at least I might eventually convince this one to teach me her trick. "Mrs. Mullins —" I started to ask, but she interrupted me.

"Allan, please, just stop asking me questions." That was the last thing she said to me all afternoon. That didn't discourage me, because I knew that when adults absolutely didn't want you to ask questions, those were the questions with the most interesting answers. And so I, Allan Hobart, the kid who'd made up his mind to get rid of this baby-sitter today, had now decided that I'd be back tormorrow for sure.

From
The Adventures of Ali Baba Bernstein
by Johanna Hurwitz

When David Bernstein gets tired of being one of four Davids in his class, he decides he needs a new name. One with pizzazz. When David changes his name to Ali Baba Bernstein, his life really starts to get exciting, just like the guy in the book he named himself after. What's in a name, anyway? Ali Baba is about to find out.

When Ali Baba Bernstein was eight years, eleven months, and four days old, his mother asked him how he wanted to celebrate his ninth birthday. He could take his friends to the bowling alley or to a movie. Or he could have a roller-skating party. None of these choices seemed very exciting to Ali Baba. Two boys in his class had already given bowling parties, another had invited all the boys in the class to a movie, and a third classmate was giving a roller-skating party next week. Ali Baba wanted to do something different.

"Do you remember when I counted all the David Bernsteins in the telephone book?"

Mrs. Bernstein nodded.

"I'd like to meet them all," said David. "I want to invite them here for my birthday."

"But you don't know them," his mother said. "And they are not your age."

"I want to see what they are all like," said Ali Baba. "If I can't invite them, then I don't want to have any party at all."

A week later, when Ali Baba was eight years, eleven months and twelve days old, his mother asked about his birthday again.

"I told you what I decided," said Ali Baba.

That night Ali Baba's parents talked about the David Bernstein party. Mr. Bernstein liked his son's idea. He thought the other David Bernsteins might be curious to meet one another. So it was agreed that Ali Baba would have the party he wanted.

The very next morning, which was Saturday, Ali Baba and his father went to his father's office. Ali Baba had written an invitation to the David Bernstein party.

Dear David Bernstein:
    I found your name in the Manhattan telephone book. My name is David Bernstein,

too. I want to meet all the David Bernsteins in New York. I am having a party on Friday, May 12th at 7:00 P.M. and I hope you can come.

My mother is cooking supper. She is a good cook.

Yours truly,
David Bernstein
(also known as Ali Baba Bernstein)

P.S. May 12th is my ninth birthday, but you don't have to bring a present. RSVP: 211-3579

Mr. Bernstein had explained that RSVP was a French abbreviation that meant please tell me if you are going to come. He also said that his son should give his age in the letter.

"Honesty is the best policy, Ali Baba," his father advised.

Ali Baba was going to use the word processor in his father's office to print the letter. It took him a long time to type his letter on the machine. His father tried to help him, but he did not type very well either. When the letter was finally completed and the print button pushed, the machine produced seventeen perfect copies — one for each David Bernstein.

That evening Ali Baba addressed the seventeen envelopes so that the invitations could be mailed on Monday morning. His father supplied the stamps. By the end of the week, two David Bernsteins had already called to accept.

By the time Ali Baba Bernstein was eight years, eleven months, and twenty-nine days old, seven David Bernsteins had accepted his invitation. Four David Bernsteins called to say they couldn't come.

Six David Bernsteins did not answer at all.

Ali Baba and his mother chose the menu for his birthday dinner. There would be pot roast, corn (Ali Baba's favorite vegetable), rolls, applesauce, and salad. They were also having kasha varnishkas (a combination of buckwheat groats and noodles), which one of the guests had requested.

The evening of the party finally arrived. Ali Baba had decided to wear a pair of slacks, a sport jacket, and real dress shoes. It was not at all the way he would have dressed for a bowling party.

Ali Baba was surprised when the first guest arrived in a jogging suit and running shoes.

"How do you do," he said when Ali Baba opened the door. "I'm David Bernstein."

"Of course," said the birthday boy. "Call me Ali Baba."

Soon the living room was filled with David Bernsteins. They ranged in age from exactly nine years and three hours old to seventy-six years old (he was the David Bernstein who had asked for kasha varnishkas). There was a television director, a delicatessen owner, a mailman, an animal groomer, a dentist, a high-school teacher, and a writer. They all lived in Manhattan now, but they had been born in Brooklyn, the Bronx, Michigan, Poland, Germany, and South Africa. None of them had ever met any of the others before.

All of the guests enjoyed the dinner. "David, will you please pass those delicious rolls," asked the mailman.

"Certainly, David," said the animal groomer on his left.

"David, would you please pass the pitcher of apple cider this way," asked the dentist.

"Here it is, David," said the television director.

"I have trouble remembering names," the seventy-six-year-old David Bernstein told Ali Baba. "At this party I can't possibly forget." He smiled at Ali Baba. "What did you say your nickname was?"

"Ali Baba is not a nickname. I have chosen it to be my real name. There are too many David Bernsteins. There were even more in the telephone book who didn't come tonight."

"I was the only David Bernstein to finish the New York City Marathon," said David Bernstein the dentist. He was the one wearing running shoes.

"The poodles I clip don't care what my name is," said David Bernstein the animal groomer.

"It's not what you're called but what you do that matters," said the seventy-six-year-old David Bernstein.

All of them agreed to that.

"I once read that in some places children are given temporary names. They call them 'milk names.' They can then choose whatever names they want when they get older," said David Bernstein the high-school teacher.

"I'd still choose David Bernstein," said David Bernstein the delicatessen owner. "Just because we all have the same name doesn't make us the same."

"You're right," agreed David Bernstein the mailman.

"Here, here," called out David Bernstein the television director. He raised his glass of apple cider. "A toast to the youngest David Bernstein in the room."

Everyone turned to Ali Baba. He was

about to say that he didn't want to be called David. But somehow he didn't mind his name so much now that he had met all these other David Bernsteins. They *were* all different. There would never be another David Bernstein like himself. One of these days he might go back to calling himself David again. But not just now.

"Open your presents," called out David Bernstein the writer.

Even though he had said that they didn't have to, several guests had brought gifts. So after singing "Happy Birthday" and cutting into the ice-cream cake that was shaped like the Manhattan phone book, Ali Baba began to open the packages. There was a pocket calculator the size of a business card, just like the one his father had. There was a jigsaw puzzle that looked like a subway map of Manhattan, a model airplane kit, and a few books. One was a collection of Sherlock Holmes stories. "I used to call myself Sherlock Bernstein," the high-school teacher recalled. There was an atlas, and, best of all, there was *The Arabian Nights*.

"Now I have my own copy!" said Ali Baba. This was the best birthday he had ever had.

Finally, it was time for the guests to leave.

"I never thought I would meet all the David Bernsteins," said David Bernstein the writer.

"You haven't," said Ali Baba. "Besides the seventeen David Bernsteins in the telephone book, there are six hundred eighty-three other Bernsteins listed between Aaron Bernstein and Zachary Bernstein. There must be members of their families who are named David. I bet there are thousands of David Bernsteins that I haven't met yet."

"You're right," said the seventy-six-year-old David Bernstein, patting Ali Baba on the back.

"Maybe I could invite them all next year," said Ali Baba. He was already nine years and six hours old.

"You could put an advertisement in the newspaper," suggested the mailman.

Ali Baba liked that idea.

David Bernstein the writer said, "I just might go home and write all about this. When did you get so interested in all the David Bernsteins?"

"It goes back a long time," said Ali Baba. "It all started on the day that I was eight years, five months, and seventeen days old."

From
Pippi Longstocking
by Astrid Lindgren

9

Almost everyone knows the lovable Pippi Longstocking with her red braids and striped socks. She is always on a hilarious adventure with her monkey — Mr. Nilsson — and her horse. When she meets her new neighbors, she invites them into her wacky world, but are they ready for Pippi?

Way out at the end of a tiny little town was an old overgrown garden, and in the garden was an old house, and in the house lived Pippi Longstocking. She was nine years old, and she lived there all alone. She had no mother and no father, and that was of course very nice because there was no one to tell her to go to bed just when she was having the most fun, and no one who could make her take cod liver oil when she much preferred caramel candy.

Once upon a time Pippi had had a father of whom she was extremely fond. Naturally she had had a mother too, but that was so long ago that Pippi didn't remember her at all. Her mother had died when Pippi was just a tiny baby and lay in a cradle and howled so that nobody could go anywhere near her. Pippi was sure that her mother was now up in Heaven, watching her little girl through a peephole in the sky, and Pippi often waved up at her and called, "Don't you worry about me. I'll always come out on top."

Her father Pippi had not forgotten. He was a sea captain who sailed on the great ocean, and Pippi had sailed with him in his ship until one day her father blew overboard in a storm and disappeared. But Pippi was absolutely certain that he would come back. She would never believe that he had drowned; she was sure he had floated until he landed on an island inhabited by cannibals. And she thought he had become the king of all the cannibals and went around with a golden crown on his head all day long.

"My papa is a cannibal king; it certainly isn't every child who has such a stylish papa," Pippi used to say with satisfaction. "And as soon as my papa has built himself a boat he will come and get me, and I'll be a cannibal princess. Heigh-ho, won't that be exciting?"

Her father had bought the old house in the

garden many years ago. He thought he would live there with Pippi when he grew old and couldn't sail the seas any longer. And then this annoying thing had to happen, that he blew into the ocean, and while Pippi was waiting for him to come back she went straight home to Villa Villekulla. That was the name of the house. It stood there ready and waiting for her. One lovely summer evening she had said good-bye to all the sailors on her father's boat. They were all so fond of Pippi, and she of them.

"So long, boys," she said and kissed each one on the forehead. "Don't you worry about me. I'll always come out on top."

Two things she took with her from the ship: a little monkey whose name was Mr. Nilsson — he was a present from her father — and a big suitcase full of gold pieces. The sailors stood up on the deck and watched as long as they could see her. She walked straight ahead without looking back at all, with Mr. Nilsson on her shoulder and her suitcase in her hand.

"A remarkable child," said one of the sailors as Pippi disappeared in the distance.

He was right. Pippi was indeed a remarkable child. The most remarkable thing about her was that she was so strong. She was so very strong that in the whole wide world there was not a single police officer who was as strong as she. Why, she could lift a whole horse if she wanted to! And she wanted to. She had a horse of her own that she had bought with one of her many gold pieces the day she came home to Villa Villekulla. She had always longed for a horse, and now here he was living on the porch. When Pippi wanted to drink her afternoon coffee there, she simply lifted him down into the garden.

Beside Villa Villekulla was another garden and another house. In that house lived a father and mother and two charming children, a boy and a girl. The boy's name was Tommy and the girl's Annika. They were good, well brought up, and obedient children. Tommy would never think of biting his nails, and he always did exactly what his mother told him to do. Annika never fussed when she didn't get her own way, and she always looked so pretty in her little well-ironed cotton dresses; she took the greatest care not to get them dirty. Tommy and Annika played nicely with each other in their garden, but they had often wished for a playmate. While Pippi was still sailing on the ocean with her father, they often used to hang over the fence and say to each other, "Isn't it silly that nobody ever moves into that house. Somebody ought to live there — somebody with children."

On that lovely summer evening when Pippi for the first time stepped over the threshold of Villa Villekulla, Tommy and Annika were not at home. They had gone to visit their grandmother for a week; and so they had no idea that anybody had moved into the house next door. On the first day after they came home again they stood by the gate, looking out onto the street, and even then they didn't know that there actually was a playmate so near. Just as they were standing there considering what they should do and wondering whether anything exciting was likely to happen or whether it was going to be one of those dull days when they couldn't think of anything to play — just then the gate of Villa Villekulla opened and a little girl stepped out. She was the most remarkable girl Tommy and Annika had ever seen. She was Miss Pippi Longstocking out for her morning promenade. This is the way she looked:

Her hair, the color of a carrot, was braided in two tight braids that stuck straight out. Her nose was the shape of a very small potato and was dotted all over with freckles. It must be admitted that the mouth under this nose was a very wide one, with strong white teeth. Her dress was rather unusual. Pippi herself had made it. She had meant it to be blue, but there wasn't quite enough blue cloth, so Pippi had sewed little red pieces on it here and there. On her long thin legs she wore a pair of long stockings, one brown and the other black; and she had on a pair of black shoes that were exactly twice as long as her feet. These shoes her father had bought for her in South America so that Pippi should have something to grow into, and she never wanted to wear any others.

But the thing that made Tommy and Annika open their eyes widest of all was the monkey sitting on the strange girl's shoulder. It was a little monkey, dressed in blue pants, yellow jacket, and a white straw hat.

Pippi walked along the street with one foot on the sidewalk and the other in the gutter. Tommy and Annika watched as long as they could see her. In a little while she came back, and now she was walking backward. That was because she didn't want to turn around to get home. When she reached Tommy's and Annika's gate she stopped.

The children looked at each other in silence. At last Tommy spoke. "Why did you walk backward?"

"Why did I walk backward?" said Pippi. "Isn't this a free country? Can't a person walk any way he wants to? For that matter, let me tell you that in Egypt everybody walks that way, and nobody thinks it's the least bit strange."

"How do you know?" asked Tommy. "You've never been in Egypt, have you?"

"I've never been in Egypt? Indeed I have. That's one thing you can be sure of. I have been all over the world and seen many things stranger than people walking backward. I wonder what you would have said if I had come along walking on my hands the way they do in Farthest India."

"Now you must be lying," said Tommy.

Pippi thought a moment. "You're right," she said sadly, "I am lying."

"It's wicked to lie," said Annika, who had at last gathered up enough courage to speak.

"Yes, it's very wicked to lie," said Pippi even more sadly. "But I forget it now and then. And how can you expect a little child whose mother is an angel and whose father is king of a cannibal island and who herself has sailed on the ocean all her life — how can you expect her to tell the truth always? And for that matter," she continued, her whole freckled face lighting up, "let me tell you that

65

in the Belgian Congo there is not a single person who tells the truth. They lie all day long. Begin at seven in the morning and keep on until sundown. So if I should happen to lie now and then, you must try to excuse me and to remember that it is only because I stayed in the Belgian Congo a little too long. We can be friends anyway, can't we?"

"Oh, sure," said Tommy and realized suddenly that this was not going to be one of those dull days.

"By the way, why couldn't you come and have breakfast with me?" asked Pippi.

"Why not?" said Tommy. "Come on, let's go."

"Oh, yes, let's," said Annika.

"But first I must introduce you to Mr. Nilsson," said Pippi, and the little monkey took off his cap and bowed politely.

Then they all went in through Villa Villekulla's tumbledown garden gate, along the gravel path, bordered with old moss-covered trees — really good climbing trees they seemed to be — up to the house, and on to the porch. There stood the horse, munching oats out of a soup bowl.

"Why do you have a horse on the porch?" asked Tommy. All horses he knew lived in stables.

"Well," said Pippi thoughtfully, "he'd be in the way in the kitchen, and he doesn't like the parlor."

Tommy and Annika patted the horse and then went on into the house. It had a kitchen, a parlor, and a bedroom. But it certainly looked as if Pippi had forgotten to do her Friday cleaning that week. Tommy and Annika looked around cautiously just in case the King of the Cannibal Isles might be sitting in a corner somewhere. They had never seen a cannibal king in all their lives. But there was no father to be seen, nor any mother either.

Annika said anxiously, "Do you live here all alone?"

"Of course not!" said Pippi. "Mr. Nilsson and the horse live here too."

"Yes, but I mean, don't you have any mother or father here?"

"No, not the least little tiny bit of a one," said Pippi happily.

"But who tells you when to go to bed at night and things like that?" asked Annika.

"I tell myself," said Pippi. "First I tell myself in a nice friendly way; and then, if I don't mind, I tell myself again more sharply; and if I still don't mind, then I'm in for a spanking — see?"

Tommy and Annika didn't see at all, but

they thought maybe it was a good way. Meanwhile they had come out into the kitchen and Pippi cried,

"Now we're going to make a pancake,
Now there's going to be a pankee,
Now we're going to fry a pankye."

Then she took three eggs and threw them up in the air. One fell down on her head and broke so that the yolk ran into her eyes, but the others she caught skillfully in a bowl, where they smashed to pieces.

"I always did hear that egg yolk was good for the hair," said Pippi, wiping her eyes. "You wait and see — mine will soon begin to grow so fast it crackles. As a matter of fact, in Brazil all the people go about with eggs in their hair. And there are no bald-headed people. Only once was there a man who was so foolish that he ate his eggs instead of rubbing them on his hair. He became completely bald-headed, and when he showed himself on the street there was such a riot that the radio police were called out."

While she was speaking Pippi had neatly picked the eggshells out of the bowl with her fingers. Now she took a bath brush that hung on the wall and began to beat the pancake

batter so hard that it splashed all over the walls. At last she poured what was left onto a griddle that stood on the stove.

When the pancake was brown on one side she tossed it halfway up to the ceiling, so that it turned right around in the air, and then she caught it on the griddle again. And when it was ready she threw it straight across the kitchen right onto a plate that stood on the table.

"Eat!" she cried. "Eat before it gets cold!"

And Tommy and Annika ate and thought it a very good pancake.

Afterward Pippi invited them to step into the parlor. There was only one piece of furniture in there. It was a huge chest with many tiny drawers. Pippi opened the drawers and showed Tommy and Annika all the treasures she kept there. There were wonderful birds' eggs, strange shells and stones, pretty little boxes, lovely silver mirrors, pearl necklaces, and many other things that Pippi and her father had bought on their journeys around the world. Pippi gave each of her new playmates a little gift to remember her by. Tommy got a dagger with a shimmering mother-of-pearl handle, and Annika a little box with a cover decorated with pink shells. In the box there was a ring with a green stone.

"Suppose you go home now," said Pippi, "so that you can come back tomorrow. Because if you don't go home you can't come back, and that would be a shame."

Tommy and Annika agreed that it would indeed. So they went home — past the horse, who had now eaten up all the oats, and out through the gate of Villa Villekulla. Mr. Nilsson waved his hat at them as they left.

*   *   *

Annika woke up early the next morning. She jumped out of bed and ran over to Tommy.

"Wake up, Tommy," she cried, pulling him

by the arm, "wake up and let's go and see that funny girl with the big shoes."

Tommy was wide awake in an instant.

"I knew, even while I was sleeping, that something exciting was going to happen to-day, but I didn't remember what it was," he said as he yanked off his pajama jacket. Off they went to the bathroom; washed them-selves and brushed their teeth much faster than usual; had their clothes on in a twin-kling; and a whole hour before their mother expected them came sliding down the ban-nister and landed at the breakfast table. Down they sat and announced that they wanted their hot chocolate right off that very moment.

From
Skylark
by Patricia MacLachlan

In the sequel to Newbery Medal–winner Sarah, Plain and Tall, *Anna and her brother, Caleb, are afraid they will have to leave the prairie they have always called home. Many have left already because of the drought. Will their new mother, Sarah, stay with them forever?*

"Stand on that stump, Caleb. Anna, you next to him. That will be a good family picture."

Joshua, the photographer, looked through his big camera at us as we stood on the porch squinting in the sunlight. Caleb wore a white shirt, his hair combed slick to his head, Sarah in a white dress, Papa looking hot and uneasy in his suit. The lace at my neck itched in the summer heat. We had to be still for so long that Caleb began to whistle softly, making Sarah smile.

Far off in the distance the dogs, Nick and Lottie, walked slowly through the dry prairie grass. They walked past the cow pond nearly empty of water, past the wagon, past the chickens in the yard. Nick saw us first, then Lottie, and they began to run. Caleb looked sideways at me as they jumped the fence and ran to us, running up to stand between Sarah and Papa as if they wanted to be in the picture, too. We tried not to laugh, but Sarah couldn't help it. She looked up at Papa and he smiled down at her. And Joshua took the picture of us all laughing, Papa smiling at Sarah.

Joshua laughed, too.

"Your aunts will like that picture," he said to Sarah.

Sarah fanned herself.

"They hardly know what I look like anymore," she said softly. "I hardly know what *they* look like anymore."

I looked at Caleb. I knew Caleb didn't like to think about Sarah and her aunts and her brother and the sea she had left behind.

"It's Maine you came from, isn't it?" said Joshua.

"Yes," said Sarah.

"She lives *here* now," said Caleb loudly.

Papa put his hand on Caleb's head.

"That she does," said Joshua, smiling.

He turned and looked out over the cornfield, the plants so dry they rattled in the wind.

"But I bet Maine is green," Joshua said in a low voice. He looked out over the land with a faraway look, as if he were somewhere else. "We sure could use rain. I remember a long time ago, you remember it, Jacob. The water dried up, the fields so dry that the leaves fell like dust. And then the winds came. My grandfather packed up his family and left."

"Did he come back?" asked Caleb.

Joshua turned.

"No," he said, "he never came back."

Joshua packed up the last of his things and got up in his wagon.

Papa looked at Sarah.

"It will rain," he said.

We watched the wagon go off down the road.

"It will rain," Papa repeated softly.

"Will you worry if it doesn't rain?" asked Caleb.

"Yes, but we'll get along," said Papa. "We always get along."

"Imagine having to *leave*," said Sarah.

Papa took off his jacket.

"We'd never leave, Sarah," he said. "We were born here. Our names are written in this land."

When Papa and Sarah went inside, Caleb

looked at me. I knew what he was going to say, and I didn't want to hear it.

"Sarah wasn't born here," he said.

I picked up the pail of grain for the chickens.

"I know that, Caleb," I said crossly. "Papa knows it, too."

Caleb took a stick and bent down in the dirt. I watched him write SARA. He looked up at me.

"I'm writing Sarah's name in the land," he said.

"You can't even spell, Caleb," I said. "You can't."

I walked away. When I turned to look at Caleb, he was staring at me. I wanted to say I was sorry for being cross with him. But I didn't.

"Happily ever after," said Caleb when Papa married Sarah. "Now we'll live happily ever after. That's what the stories say."

Caleb said that all through the summer and the fall when the prairie grasses turned yellow, and through the first winter Sarah and Papa were married. He said it all winter long, when the wind blew around the corners of the house and ice sat slick on the windows. He said it when he fell through the ice on the slough and had to sit in a tub of warm water, his teeth chattering.

"I like the sound of it," Caleb told me. "Happily ever after."

* * *

The days grew hotter, the sun beating down on us. We stayed inside as much as we could. Even Nick and Lottie stayed inside, stretched out on the wood floor to keep cool. Papa walked the fields, measuring the level of the water in the well over and over, waiting for rain. He came in bringing the dirt with him.

"Papa!" I poked at his feet with my broom. "Your boots!"

I was sweeping, trying to keep the dust out. Sarah was scrubbing the kitchen floor on her hands and knees.

Papa was hot and tired.

"That may be the last washing for the floor," he said to Sarah. "We have to save water."

"That's a mixed blessing," Sarah said, brushing the hair off her face. She watched Caleb feed Seal.

"Don't feed her too much, Caleb," said Sarah. "She's getting fat with your food."

Papa looked closely at Seal. "I think she's more than fat, Sarah."

Sarah looked up. "What?"

"What does he mean?" asked Caleb.

I smiled.

"Kittens. He means kittens, Caleb," I said.

Caleb and I spoke at the same time.

"Can we keep them all?" I asked.

"When will she have them, Papa?" asked Caleb, excited.

"Don't know, Caleb," said Papa, drinking water from the tin cup.

Sarah sat back.

"Has she ever had kittens before, Sarah?" asked Papa.

Sarah shook her head.

"No, never."

Papa smiled at Sarah's look. She stared at Seal for a long time.

"Kittens," she said, her face suddenly breaking into a smile. "Kittens!"

Late light fell across the bedroom, the windows closed to the prairie wind.

I held Sarah's wedding dress up to me and looked in the mirror.

"Anna?"

I jumped, startled, and Sarah smiled at me.

"I didn't mean to frighten you," she said.

I looked in the mirror again.

"Someday I'll marry and move to my husband's land. That's what Papa says."

"Oh he does, does he?" said Sarah.

"That's what you did, Sarah. You came from Maine to marry Papa," I told her.

Sarah was silent for a moment. She sat on the bed.

"Yes," she said slowly. "I guess I did."

"You fell in love with us," said Caleb in the doorway.

"I did that," she said. "First your letters. Then you."

"Did you fall in love with Papa's letters, too? Before you knew him?" asked Caleb.

I sat on the bed and watched Sarah's face as she remembered.

"Yes, I loved your Papa's letters," said Sarah softly. "I loved what was between the lines most."

"What was between the lines?" Caleb asked.

Sarah looked at me when she answered.

"His life," she said simply. "That was what was between the lines."

"Papa's not always good with words," I said.

"Sometimes, yes," said Sarah, laughing. "But when I read your Papa's letters, I could see this farm, and the animals and the sky. And you. Sometimes, what people choose to write down on paper is more important than what they say."

Caleb didn't know what Sarah meant. But I knew. I wrote in my journal every night. And when I read what I had written, I could see myself there, clearer than when I looked in the mirror. I could see all of us: Papa, who couldn't always say the things he felt; Caleb, who said everything; and Sarah, who didn't know that she had changed us all.

From
Fourth Grade Is a Jinx
by Colleen O'Shaughnessy McKenna

9

Collette Murphy is excited to finally be a fourth-grader. But the person who thinks she's Collette's new best friend is the rudest, snobbiest, most annoying girl in the whole class. When her real best friend, Sarah, needs her most, will Collette be able to come through for her?

"Wasn't it nice of Mrs. Johnston to let us have time in school to cover our books?" asked Collette. She opened her desk and laid her science book on top of a neatly stacked pile. "Fourth grade is going to be such a great year!"

"Great?" moaned Marsha, slumping three inches deeper in her chair. "What's so great about being forced to do all this work on the very first day of school?"

Collette looked at the clutter on Marsha's desk top and started to laugh.

"I don't see what's so funny, Collette. I still have four more books to cover, and I'm already worn out from that long math ditto we had to do this morning."

"I'll cover two books for you, Marsha."

Collette picked up a glossy cover and started to fold it over Marsha's speller.

Marsha sat up straighter and tried to smooth down her bangs. She was always pushing them straight up in the air when she got upset.

"You're so nice, Collette. Maybe you can be my best friend this year in school."

Collette tried not to frown. She bent her head over the speller and busied herself with folding and taping.

She had known Marsha for years and years, since kindergarten. They lived right across the street from each other, which is why they were friends at all.

But they certainly couldn't be called best friends. They were much, much too different from each other.

Best friends were special, almost holy. You certainly didn't call anyone your best friend unless you really meant it.

Collette looked to the back of the classroom at Sarah, her real, true, best friend.

Ever since the beginning of third grade they had been close. Sarah was special. She never went out of her way to get Collette mad over something, like Marsha did. In fact, Sarah was always checking to make sure Collette was having just as much fun as she was.

Sarah was an only child, just like Marsha. But she didn't go around bragging about it like it meant you were of royal blood. Marsha seemed to think the more children in a family, the less fancy the family.

Collette gave Sarah a small wave and smiled when Sarah waved back. Having a best friend in the classroom was almost as nice as being home.

"I was hoping my mom would break down and send me to Shadywood Academy this year," complained Marsha. "But here I am again, back at old fuddy-duddy Sacred Heart Elementary."

Marsha slapped her hand down on her desk and raised her eyes upward like she was praying.

"I mean, let's face it. My parents can certainly afford to send me anywhere in the city. We have money coming out of our ears!"

Looking across the desk, Collette gave a slight scowl. Maybe she didn't have as much money as Marsha, but at least she knew it was rude to talk about it.

"So I guess I'm stuck in this boring plaid uniform for another year," continued Marsha.

Collette looked down at her own uniform. She touched the small red diamond with the navy stitching of Sacred Heart printed neatly in the center.

Her jumper wasn't the least bit boring. Especially now that she was in the fourth grade and wore a size ten. Size-ten jumpers came with a pocket.

"They aren't so bad, Marsha," said Collette loyally.

She stacked Marsha's speller on top of the jumbled pile and reached for the social studies book. "Our jumpers are much nicer than the ones they wear at St. John's Academy."

"Oh, you," pouted Marsha. She blew the left side of her bangs up in the air. "You're easy to please because you don't have a million dollars' worth of clothes hanging in your closet like I do. Anyway, the plaid looks better on you with your blonde hair. But with my dark good looks, plaid makes me look drab."

Marsha made a fist and blew up the other side of her bangs. Once Marsha's forehead was showing, you knew she was working herself up into a rage.

"Nine years old is too young to be drab!" she finally exploded.

"Marsha!" laughed Sarah as she came running over. "What are you so upset about?"

Sarah reached out and tugged gently on Collette's ponytail. Collette grinned back, glad that Sarah noticed that her hair was finally long enough for a real ponytail.

"Boy, your desk is a mess, Marsha," observed Sarah. "What have you been doing all day?"

"Everything! Come on, Sarah. Cover a book for me, please?" begged Marsha miserably. "I don't know why teachers can't cover these for us over the summer. What do they do with their time off?"

Collette and Sarah looked at each other with raised eyebrows. They tried not to smile. Once Marsha's bangs were up, she lost her temper very easily.

"If we hurry, we can go to the back of the room and get one of the free reading books," reminded Sarah. "I was helping Mrs. Johnston set them up. Boy, does she have a lot of them!"

"We never had our own library in the third grade," added Collette. She held the social studies book out to Marsha. "All finished. Come on, let's go get a book before they're all taken."

"Wait for me," whined Marsha, wrestling with a wrinkled folder.

"Slow down, Marsha," said Roger. He walked slowly past her desk, balancing a book on his fingertip. "There's nothing back there for you, anyway."

Collette looked from Marsha to Roger, waiting. Roger teased all of the girls, especially Marsha, because she got the maddest the fastest.

"Why?" demanded Marsha as she tossed the last book into the jungle within her desk. "Were you rude, taking them all, Mr. Friday?"

Roger just smiled and shook his head. "No, but all the coloring books are still down in the first grade . . . where you belong."

Sarah nudged Collette lightly with her shoe and nodded toward Marsha. It was easy to see Marsha was getting ready to attack. She kept twisting a clump of hair around and around her index finger.

"Five more minutes till lunch," announced Mrs. Johnston from the front of the room.

"I just lost my appetite, thanks to Roger," muttered Marsha as she stomped back to the bookshelves.

"My dad packed my lunch this morning,"

said Sarah. "I can hardly wait to see what he packed me."

"Your father?" asked Collette. "Your mother is the fancy cook in your house. I thought she would make you cute little cucumber sandwiches to celebrate the first day of school."

"Not today. But my mom may end up being a famous cook. Remember that cookbook she had been working on?"

Collette nodded.

"Well, she sent it off a couple months ago and now someone in New York wants to publish it. She flew up there this morning to talk to them about stuff. She'll be gone for two days."

"New York?" Collette paused, studying Sarah's face. Was Sarah excited about her mom's book, or lonely already because her mom left for New York without her?

"Listen, Sarah, you can have half my sandwich if your dad packed you something disgusting, like sardines," offered Collette. "In fact, my mom wouldn't mind packing your whole lunch until your mom gets back. She already does three lunches — one more won't matter."

Sarah started to laugh. "Thanks, but my

dad knows how to pack a lunch. I do, too, probably. Besides, my mom left lots of charts and directions about everything taped to the refrigerator."

Collette nodded, taking a step closer and lowering her voice.

"But who is going to take care of you after school, Sarah? Is your dad allowed to leave the bank early?"

Reaching down into the neck of her blouse, Sarah drew out a thin silver chain. On the end dangled a key.

"A key?" sputtered Collette. "You mean you'll . . . you'll be watching yourself?"

Sarah blushed. She shrugged her shoulders and dropped the key back down her blouse.

"It's only for an hour or two after school, Collette. I made myself some peanut butter and crackers this morning. I can eat those for a snack and read a book."

Collette nodded. What could she say? Poor Sarah! She had no idea how lonely she was going to be in her apartment. She didn't even have rooms full of brothers and a little sister, like Collette.

Sarah didn't even have a dog!

"Don't mention the key to anyone," cautioned Sarah. "My parents don't want me to broadcast the fact that I'll be alone."

"Who's going to be alone?" asked Marsha as she joined them.

Sarah lifted her key.

"Oh, you lucky dog." Marsha sounded jealous. "I wish I had my own key."

"Sarah, I have a great idea," cried Collette, brightening suddenly. "Come home with me after school. Your dad could pick you up on the way from the bank. I'm sure my mother wouldn't mind you being there!"

"Mind?" interrupted Marsha. "Your house is already so crammed with little kids, your mom wouldn't even find Sarah for a day or two."

Marsha gave a smug little laugh before she reached out and snatched Sarah's arm. "Come home with me, Sarah. Since we're both *only* children, you'll feel more at home at my house. We can make popcorn in my microwave and relax in front of our VCR."

Collette sighed. Her house could never compete with Marsha's. Marsha had more fancy gadgets in her bedroom than Collette had in her whole house.

Collette still had to share a bedroom with her five-year-old sister, Laura. The two of them shared a Big Bird alarm clock.

Sarah probably thought they were Amish.

"I'll be fine," laughed Sarah. "My mom

wants me to get used to this, anyway. She'll be taking more and more little trips to promote her book. She's so excited about this cookbook."

Collette took in a deep breath. Sarah was so brave, so cheerful about her mom up and leaving town.

Fourth grade must sound a whole lot older to Sarah's parents. They never left Sarah without a baby-sitter in the third grade.

"Hey, I'll call you as soon as I get home, okay, Collette?" Sarah was patting Collette's arm, whispering so Marsha wouldn't hear. "I'm used to being alone. Lots of times my parents are in the living room, reading, and I stay in my bedroom, watching T.V. or —"

"Oh, sure," Collette broke in. She tried to sound real positive and perky. She didn't want Sarah to think she was feeling sorry for her. Besides, it wasn't as though Collette's parents were thinking about leaving Collette alone after school for hours at a time. Her mother had never had an extra key made for Collette.

Right now, there were too many little Murphys running around who needed a lot of watching. Stevie was only three, and Laura had just started kindergarten. And even though Jeff was trying to act like a cool kid all of a sudden, he was still only seven. Even cool seven-year-olds needed someone to drive them to soccer and make them a fried egg sandwich.

Looking up from her desk, Collette smiled bravely back at Sarah. There was nothing left to do now but to stand by Sarah the best way she could. That's what best friends were for.

And as soon as she got home from school she would explain things to her mother. Her mother was great at solving things. No problem was too tough for her. She would probably call Sarah's dad at the bank and cheerfully insist that Sarah come home with Collette whenever Mrs. Messland had to be out of town.

Everyone knew how much Mrs. Murphy liked kids. Sarah's dad would laugh back and say, "Sure thing. Now why didn't I think of that?"

As soon as Mrs. Johnston announced lunch, Collette stood up and smiled. Fourth grade with Mrs. Johnston was going to be a great year. Probably the best year of all!

Being Nine Is Just Fine
by Patricia C. McKissack

Michael is so proud to have a friend who is ten years old. But sometimes Tyrell is mean to Michael's other friends. When Tyrell goes too far, will Michael be brave enough to speak up? With this original story, Patricia C. McKissack, winner of the Newbery Honor and Coretta Scott King Award, gives readers a special lesson.

Michael was very impressed with Tyrell, the new boy at school. Tyrell was stronger, taller, and faster than anybody in Mrs. Mason's fourth-grade class. And even more, Tyrell had turned ten already, making him older than Michael and his friends, who were still in single digits.

"All of my friends are older than you," Tyrell told Michael. "But you seem to be an a'right nine, so I'll let you hang with me."

Michael was thrilled. Nothing could beat being nine and having a friend who was ten.

"If you gon' be down with me, though, you got to do what I say do, when I say do it. Got that?"

"That's cool," Michael answered without really thinking.

The two boys began spending all their free time together. Whatever Tyrell wanted to do, Michael agreed. Wherever Tyrell wanted to go, Michael followed. Within days Michael had changed the way he walked, the way he talked, and the way he treated his other friends.

Tyrell wouldn't eat at the same lunch table with all the other fourth-graders, saying, "If you hang with me, you can't be with those nerds."

Michael wanted to impress Tyrell, so he went along and followed Tyrell to a table where they sat by themselves.

Out on the playground, Tyrell said he didn't like silly games, so they sat and watched the others play kickball. Malik ran over and flopped down beside them. He asked Michael for help with his math homework.

"No, he won't," Tyrell said, not giving Michael a chance to answer. "Not unless you pay him five dollars."

Malik's eyes stretched wide. Michael and

he had studied together since they were in kindergarten. It had always been fun. "Pay?" he exclaimed in disbelief. "I don't think so —"

Before Malik could finish, Tyrell was in his face. "No more freebies. Do your own homework. Now, pay up or shut up!"

Malik looked at Michael with sad dark eyes, as if waiting for his friend to say something. But Michael looked at the ground and dug a hole with his heel. "Tyrell is right," he said at last. "No more free help. You got to pay."

"You wish," said Malik, walking away in disgust.

All day Michael felt like a stone had settled in the pit of his stomach. But he couldn't figure out why he felt so awful.

Tyrell didn't like riding in the park, skateboarding, or playing baseball. So Michael stopped doing those things, too.

After school, a group of kids were out on the playground playing soccer. "What does Tyrell like to do?" Michael's classmates asked.

"He likes video games," the boy explained. What he didn't tell them was that Tyrell liked playing the same one over and over. "Tyrell doesn't like playing with anybody but me."

"Wrong!" said Malik. "Nobody will play with Tyrell except you, Michael."

Just then Tyrell approached the group. He glared at everybody and refused to speak.

"Come on, let's go to the library," someone suggested.

Tyrell turned his nose up like he smelled something bad. "Nobody but geeks go to the library. No friend of mine would be caught reading a book," Tyrell said, jamming his hands in his pockets and sauntering across the street.

"Right," Michael chimed in, following behind Tyrell step for step. But the rock in his stomach was getting heavier and heavier.

"Where'd you get that dumb idea?" Sharonda called after them. "Michael, you love to read!"

Tyrell stopped and glared at her with angry eyes. "Who you calling dumb?"

"Yeah," added Michael, "watch who you call dumb."

"I know exactly who I'm calling dumb! You, Tyrell, for being a real snot rag, and you, Michael, for following him around like a puppy."

The next morning Michael had forgotten about what Sharonda had said, but not Tyrell. "Nobody calls me dumb and gets away with it."

"Sharonda's always saying stuff. She

doesn't mean it," Michael tried to explain. Tyrell wasn't listening. His mind was on getting even. Tyrell shared his plan. Michael thought it was like a practical joke — nothing to hurt anybody. So he agreed to help.

After the weekly true-or-false science quiz, Mrs. Mason asked for the papers to be passed forward. That's when the plan went into action. Michael got Sharonda's attention. Meanwhile, Tyrell switched the names on his and Sharonda's papers.

When the tests were returned after lunch, Sharonda got a big red F. Tyrell got all the answers correct. Sharonda was almost in tears. Even though she tried, she couldn't convince Mrs. Mason that it wasn't her paper. Sharonda hadn't looked that hurt and confused since she lost her coat in kindergarten.

When was Tyrell going to say that it was all a joke? Michael wondered. Tyrell never said a word. He kept Sharonda's A, while she was stuck with an F — Tyrell's F.

"Did you see her face when she saw that F?" Tyrell said, laughing when they went out for afternoon recess.

Michael didn't feel like laughing. He was thinking about what he had done to his good friend. "Maybe we should tell Mrs. Mason that it was all a joke, so —"

Suddenly, Tyrell stopped laughing. He narrowed his eyes. He looked like a giant standing over Michael. "I thought we were tight," Tyrell said through clenched teeth. "I've got your back and you've got mine! Right?"

"Right . . ." Michael wanted to say more, but he didn't want his new friend to think he was a geek.

Over the next few days, Tyrell demanded more and more of Michael's time, so Michael saw less and less of his old friends. On Saturday, Malik and Sharonda and a few other kids from the neighborhood stopped by Michael's house. He and Tyrell were sitting on the steps doing nothing.

"Come ride in the bikeathon to help raise money for the Children's Hospital Burn Center," Malik said.

Michael was ready to go, but Tyrell answered for them. "Why would we ride and get all sweaty to raise money for people we don't even know?"

"Because it's fun and it's helping somebody," said Sharonda.

"Sounds nerdy to me," Tyrell said, leaning back again on the step.

"Are you sure you don't want to go with us, Michael? You did last year," said Malik.

It was a bright March day, just warm

enough for a jacket. Not a cloud in the sky. It had been so long since Michael had ridden his bike and felt the wind blowing in his face. But Tyrell said doing stuff like that was weird. Michael wanted to be with his friends, but he just couldn't. "No, you go on. I — I'll check you guys later," he said, leaning back on the step like Tyrell.

When they were alone, Michael decided to speak up . . . a little. "I'm bored," he said. "Can't we *do* something?"

Tyrell looked surprised. "Like what?"

"I know it's cool just hanging out, but don't you think we could do something else besides watch television and play that same video game all the time?" Michael didn't know what to expect, but it wasn't what happened next.

Suddenly, Tyrell sprang to his feet. "Yeah! I know something we can do. Look out for me," he whispered.

Michael couldn't believe it when Tyrell ran to the curb, reached inside Mr. Kellerman's car window, and turned on the lights. "Hey," Michael said, "that'll run down the battery!"

"This will teach the old man a good lesson for leaving his car windows open. Ought to be glad somebody didn't steal it. Next time maybe he'll lock up." Tyrell was bent over laughing.

Michael didn't know what to say, but he knew what to do. Pushing past Tyrell, he reached inside and shut off the lights. "Mr. Kellerman's old and he forgets sometimes."

"Hey, there," Mr. Kellerman yelled from across the street. "What are you kids doing in my car?"

Tyrell ducked out of sight. Michael didn't. He waved at Mr. Kellerman. "It's me, sir, Michael Temple. I was just shutting your car lights off and locking your door."

Mr. Kellerman smiled. "Thanks, Michael. I do forget things these days. You're a good kid."

Michael didn't feel like a good kid, especially when Tyrell praised him, saying, "You're a'right for a nine-year-old. You didn't get all scared and tattle at the first sign of trouble." Michael wasn't comfortable with Tyrell's kind of joking around. It made him feel worse than he already did.

Monday was a field trip day. Mrs. Mason took the class to see the new shark exhibit at the science museum. Half the class went through the display while the other half saw a movie. Michael's group was taken to the section where there were life-sized models of sharks.

"Please don't touch anything," said the guide. "These skeleton replicas are very delicate."

Tyrell whispered to Michael, "Let's play a trick on Malik."

Michael wanted to stop him, but it was too late. Tyrell slipped away, carefully ducked under the guard rope, and took a shark's tooth from the model. Michael watched silently as Tyrell put the tooth in Malik's pocket.

The guide moved the group to the next display. "Yieeks!" he cried out in alarm. "A tooth is missing from the tiger sharks model."

Tyrell stepped forward. "Sir, I know who did it." All the class looked surprised. Who was Tyrell going to name? "Malik has it!" he shouted.

Poor Malik looked like he'd been attacked by a real shark. "I didn't take anything," he said, trying not to look too frightened.

"Admit it," Tyrell insisted. "I saw him put something in his pocket. You saw it, too, didn't you, Michael?" Tyrell winked.

Michael felt like the stone in his stomach weighed a ton.

Speak up, say something, Michael heard the small voice of his conscience say. But he was afraid of looking like a nerd, a geek, a creep — all the things Tyrell called people if they didn't act or think like him.

"Do you have the tooth?" the guide asked Malik.

"No, sir, I don't," Malik said, reaching in his pocket.

The guide hurried away to get Mrs. Mason. He didn't see the look on Malik's face when the boy felt the tooth in his pocket.

Malik showed it to everybody. "I didn't take this," he said. "But Mrs. Mason isn't going to believe me."

"She sure won't," said Tyrell. "We all saw you take it out of your pocket."

"I don't care what," said Sharonda. "If Malik says he didn't take it, I believe him." Other classmates joined in.

"We believe you, Malik."

"Malik was standing by me all the time. Somebody must have put it in his pocket," Sharonda said, looking at Tyrell.

"Hey, you all saw it. Malik took the tooth out of his pocket right here in front of you. And when Mrs. Mason comes back that's what we're going to tell her, aren't we, Michael?"

Michael swallowed hard. What could he do? What could he say? Then he knew. "I believe you, Malik," he said, taking the shark's tooth from Malik's hand.

Tyrell looked confused for a moment, then he snapped his finger. "That's it. Michael was the one. He put the tooth in Malik's pocket."

"Tyrell, shut up," said Michael.

Everybody started slapping hands and cheering. "We've been waiting for you to tell him that for weeks," said Sharonda. Everybody agreed.

Tyrell was furious. He narrowed his eyes and clenched his fists. "You little chump," he said, snarling at Michael.

But Michael stood toe-to-toe with him. "Malik didn't take that tooth. Neither did I. You did!"

Then to everybody's amazement, Tyrell's expression changed. He looked scared and bewildered. "I-I thought we were friends, Michael," he whined. "You're not going to rat on me, are you?"

Michael blinked in surprise. "No, I-I-I hadn't planned to tell," he said.

"If I get into trouble, my dad will hang me. Please don't tell."

Tyrell was taller, stronger, and faster than

every kid in class, but in the blink of an eye, he seemed so much younger than they were. "Hey, chill. I'm not telling. But you've got to make things right," Michael said.

"Okay," said Tyrell, taking the tooth from Michael and putting it back in place. "Just please don't tell. One more thing. We've got to fix the dirty trick we did with Sharonda's science paper."

Sharonda gasped. She put her hands on her hips and moved in close to Tyrell. "You're the one! I knew you had something to do with it. And Michael, you didn't say a thing."

Tyrell shrugged. "What can I do?" he whined some more.

"You thought of the trick, now think of a way to undo it," said Michael.

Mrs. Mason and a security guard came back. The tooth was in place and nobody said a word. Mrs. Mason was relieved everything was back where it belonged. And so was everybody else.

At lunch the next day, Michael was back at the table with all his classmates. "Welcome back!" said Malik.

"Thanks for getting Tyrell to convince Mrs. Mason to let me take the science test over again," Sharonda said, offering half her peanut butter and jelly sandwich to Michael.

"Tyrell can be really convincing," he said, smiling.

"We know," said Malik. "I'm sure glad you're not friends with him anymore."

"Wrong!" said Michael. "Tyrell doesn't want to be friends with *me* anymore. What he needs is a real friend — one who will speak up sooner."

Just then, Tyrell and a third-grader passed their table. "Nerds," Tyrell hissed.

"Nerds," the eight-year-old mimicked, trying to walk and talk like the ten-year-old.

Michael laughed. "You know, I did learn something from Tyrell that is good."

"Tell us?" his friends asked in unison.

"Being nine is just fine!"

From
The Hoboken Chicken Emergency
by Daniel Pinkwater

❾

What is a chicken emergency? For Arthur Bobowicz it's when his family is trying hard to be American and have a turkey like everyone else for Thanksgiving. But all the turkeys are sold out, so they will have to settle for a chicken — a 266-pound chicken! Don't ask, just read on. . . .

Nobody in Arthur Bobowicz's family really liked turkey. Certainly, the kids didn't like it as much as chicken or duck. They suspected that Momma and Poppa didn't like it very much either. Still, they had a turkey every Thanksgiving, like almost every family in Hoboken. "Thanksgiving is an important American holiday," Poppa would say. "You kids are Americans, and you ought to celebrate important American holidays. On Thanksgiving, you eat turkey. Would you want people to think you were ungrateful?" Poppa came from Poland, and he was very big on holidays, and being an

American. There was no arguing with him. They had turkey every year.

Most of the kids in the neighborhood had the same scene at home. Some of them liked turkey, some of them didn't — but they all had it on Thanksgiving. They all had fathers like Arthur Bobowicz's father — they came from Italy, and the Ukraine, and Puerto Rico, and Hong Kong. The kids were all being raised to be Americans, and everyone's father knew that Americans eat turkey on Thanksgiving. Late in November, in the windows of the stores in Hoboken, where ducks had hung, and sausages, and legs of lamb — turkeys appeared. For the rest of the year, anyone who wanted a turkey would have had to go clear out of town. The turkeys appeared in Hoboken at Thanksgiving, no other time.

It was Arthur's job to go and get the family turkey. Poppa had reserved a turkey weeks in advance at Murphy's Meat Market. On Thanksgiving morning, Arthur was supposed to go to the market and bring back the turkey, a big one. The whole family was going to be there — uncles and aunts, and some cousins, Momma and Poppa, and Arthur's little brother and sister. Bringing back the turkey was an important job. Once it came into the house, all the cooking and rushing out for

last-minute things from the store, and all the good smells would start. It was a good holiday, and all the kids enjoyed it — but it would have been even better if they had a duck or a chicken.

Something had gone wrong at Murphy's Meat Market. Somehow Poppa's turkey reservation had gotten lost. Every turkey had some family's name on it — none of them had the name Bobowicz. Arthur ran down Garden Street and up the stairs of the apartment house. He told his mother about the mistake at the meat market. "Maybe you'd better go back and get two chickens and a duck," his mother said. She was almost smiling, "I'll explain it to your father." Arthur was sure she didn't like turkey either — why wouldn't she admit it?

Things had gone even more wrong than Arthur thought. When he got back to Murphy's Meat Market, there wasn't a single chicken in the place — no ducks either. All they had were turkeys, and every one of them was reserved for somebody else. Arthur was bothered by this, but not terribly worried. There are lots of stores and markets in Hoboken — German and Italian butchers, Spanish groceries, supermarkets. You can get almost anything to eat in the world in Hoboken —

except a turkey, a chicken, or a duck on Thanksgiving, as Arthur found out. He went to every store in town that might possibly have a bird. He went to a few stores that probably did not have birds — just in case. "This is a fish market! What makes you think we'd have turkeys or chickens, you silly kid?"

"No chickens in a vegetable store, you silly kid!"

"Silly kid! This is an Indian spice store. Curry powder, we've got; mango chutney, we've got; flash-frozen chapatis, we've got — birds we do not have."

Arthur was looking for turkeys, chickens, ducks, geese — he would have taken any kind of bird at all. There wasn't anything of the kind to be found in the whole town. It was getting to be late in the morning, and it was snowing a little. Arthur was getting depressed. This was the first time he had the job of getting the Thanksgiving bird, and he had messed it up. He had tried everyplace; he had sixteen dollars in his pocket, and he hadn't found one single bird. He walked along River Street. He didn't want to go home and tell his mother the bad news. He felt tired, and the cold was going right through him. He noticed a card stuck in the window of an apartment house door:

PROFESSOR MAZZOCCHI
INVENTOR OF THE CHICKEN SYSTEM
BY APPOINTMENT

Arthur rang the bell. What did he have to lose? The door-buzzer buzzed, and he pushed it open. He stood at the bottom of the stairs. A voice from above shouted, "You will not get me evicted! My brother owns this building! I am a scientist! If you people don't stop bothering me, I'll let the rooster loose again!"

"Do you have a chicken for sale?" Arthur shouted — he was desperate.

"What? You want to buy a chicken? Come right up!" the voice from above answered. Arthur climbed the stairs. At the head of the stairs was an old man. He was wearing an old bathrobe with dragons embroidered on it. "I have been waiting for years for someone to come to buy a superchicken," the old man said. "The only people who ever come here are neighbors to complain about my chickens. They don't want me to keep them."

"You keep chickens in your apartment?" Arthur asked.

"A farm would be better," Professor Mazzocchi said, "but my brother lets me stay here without paying any rent. Also they are special chickens. I prefer to keep them under lock and key."

"We need one to cook for Thanksgiving," Arthur said.

"A large family?" Professor Mazzocchi asked. "All my cousins are coming," Arthur said.

"And how much money did you bring?" the old man asked, "sixteen dollars? Good. Wait here." The old man went inside the apartment with Arthur's sixteen dollars. When he opened the door, Arthur heard a clucking sound, but not like any clucking he had ever heard — it was deeper, louder. Arthur had a feeling that this wasn't going to work out.

He was right. Professor Mazzocchi came out of the apartment a few minutes later. He was leading a chicken that was taller than he was. "This is the best poultry bargain on earth," he said, "a medium sized super-chicken — six cents a pound — here's your two hundred and sixty-six pound chicken, on the hoof. She'll be mighty good eating. Please don't forget to return the leash and collar," and Professor Mazzocchi closed the apartment door.

Arthur stood on the landing with the giant chicken for a while. The chicken looked bored. She shifted from foot to foot, and stared at nothing with her little red eyes. Arthur was trying to understand what had just happened. He was trying to believe there was a two hundred and sixty-six pound chicken standing in the hallway with him. Arthur was feeling numb.

Then Arthur found himself pounding on Professor Mazzocchi's door. "No refunds!" Professor Mazzocchi shouted, without opening the door.

"Don't you have anything smaller?" Arthur shouted.

"No refunds!" Professor Mazzocchi, Inventor of the Chicken System, shouted. Arthur could see that this was all he was going to get from Professor Mazzocchi. He picked up the end of the leash.

"She is a bargain, when you consider the price per pound." Arthur thought. The chicken tamely followed Arthur down the stairs.

Everybody noticed the chicken as Arthur led it home. Most people didn't want to get too close to it. Some people made a sort of moaning noise when they saw the chicken. Arthur and the chicken arrived at the apartment house where the Bobowicz family lived.

Arthur led the chicken up the stairs and tied the leash to the bannister. Then he went in to prepare his mother. "That took a long time," she said, "did you get a bird?"

"I got a chicken," Arthur said.

"Well, where is it?" his mother asked.

"I left it in the hall," Arthur said. "It only cost six cents a pound."

"That's very cheap," his mother said. "Are you sure there's nothing wrong with it? Maybe it isn't fresh."

"It's fresh," Arthur said. "It's alive."

"You brought home a live chicken?" his mother was getting excited.

"It was the only one I could find." Arthur started to cry. "I went to all the stores, and nobody had any turkeys or chickens or ducks, and finally I bought this chicken from an old man who raises them in his apartment."

Arthur's mother was headed for the door, "Momma, it's a very big chicken!" Arthur shouted. She opened the door. The chicken was standing there, shifting from foot to foot, blinking.

"CLUCK," it said. Arthur's mother closed the door, and just stood staring at it. She didn't say anything for a long time.

Finally she said, "There's a two hundred pound chicken in the hall." She was talking to the door.

"Two hundred and sixty-six pounds," Arthur said; he was still sobbing.

"Two hundred and sixty-six pounds of live chicken," his mother said. "It's wearing a dog collar."

"I'm supposed to return that," Arthur said. Arthur's mother opened the door and peeked out. Then she closed the door again. She looked at Arthur. She opened the door and looked at the chicken.

"She seems friendly, in a dumb way," she said.

"I thought we could call her Henrietta," Arthur said. "You were supposed to bring home an ordinary chicken to eat," Arthur's mother said. "Not a two hundred and sixty-six pound chicken to keep as a pet."

"It was the only one I could find," Arthur said.

Arthur's little brother and sister had been watching all this from behind the kitchen door. "Please let us keep her," they shouted, "we'll help Arthur feed her, and walk her, and take care of her."

"She walks on the leash very nicely," Arthur said. "I can train her, and she can cluck if burglars ever come. She's a good chicken, PLEASE!"

"Put her in the kitchen, and we'll discuss it when your father comes home," Arthur's mother said.

That night the family had meatloaf, and mashed potatoes, and vegetables for Thanksgiving dinner. Everybody thought it was a good meal. Henrietta especially liked the mashed potatoes, although Poppa warned everybody not to feed her from the table. "I don't want this chicken to get into the habit of begging," he said, "and the first time the children forget to feed or walk her — out she goes."

Poppa had decided to let Arthur keep Henrietta. "Every boy should have a chicken," he said.

From
The Flunking of Joshua T. Bates
by Susan Shreve

Joshua has trouble reading, so much that the worst possible thing has happened — he has to repeat third grade! Joshua tries to think of everything to get out of being a third-grader again, even moving to East Africa. But Joshua's new teacher, Mrs. Goodwin, seems pretty cool. She doesn't treat him like he's dumb. Maybe there are worse things than flunking after all.

Mrs. Goodwin was a small, square woman with curly gray hair, thick, wire-rimmed glasses, and a serious face which at that moment seemed to Joshua fierce enough to wipe out a battalion of metal soldiers with a single glance.

"I'm Joshua Bates," he said.

"I know," she replied, shaking his hand.

On the bulletin board behind Mrs. Goodwin's desk, there was a sign painted in bright colors: WELCOME TO THIRD GRADE.

"I suppose you know that I've been in third grade once already," Joshua said as he sat on the edge of one of the desks.

"Today is the worst day in my life," he added combatively, hoping she would consider herself at fault.

"Mine too," Mrs. Goodwin said matter-of-factly as she wrote the date on the blackboard. Joshua wanted immediately to ask her why, thinking perhaps it was his arrival in the third grade that had ruined her life as well as his, but the other children were beginning to arrive so he said nothing. He slid into one of the desks in the front of the room, took a pencil and paper out of his bookbag, and appeared to be hard at work on cartoon drawings of *Star Wars* figures. He hoped no one would recognize him.

"That's a good place for you to sit so I can keep an eye on you," Mrs. Goodwin said as she placed a red reading book titled *The Joy of Reading: 3* on his desk.

Joshua didn't bother to tell Mrs. Goodwin that he wasn't going to be around to keep an eye on. She'd find out soon enough.

Instead he looked at *The Joy of Reading*, which was the same book Mrs. Nice had made him read one terrible day after the next.

117

"I've had this book already," he said. "I know these stories by heart."

Mrs. Goodwin looked at him crossly over her wire-rimmed glasses.

"Recite them," she said.

"Not by heart exactly. You know what I mean." He leaned back in his chair and with his eyes closed, he imagined the pleasure of throwing the warm, soft tomatoes rotting in his mother's garden at Mrs. Goodwin's gray print dress.

The classroom began to fill with children whose faces were familiar to Joshua from the playground but whose names he did not know, of course, since it was a matter of principle at Mirch Elementary to know only the names of the older children, never the younger ones. These children were smaller than Joshua had imagined possible. He felt like a huge, dumb grizzly bear, he told Amanda later. Not one of these third graders came to his shoulder.

At the desk next to him was the smallest girl Joshua had ever seen in grade school, or so she seemed. She had pale pink cheeks, tight yellow curls, and a foolish-looking dress with aqua hippopotamuses all over it.

"Are you actually in third grade?" he asked her. Certainly he wasn't going to spend

the year with a girl so young that she still wore zoo animals on her dresses.

"Of course, dummy," she said quite pleasantly. "I remember you from last year. You've been in third grade once already."

"No kidding," the boy in back of her said. "Did you flunk or something? I have a cousin who flunked third grade twice."

"I didn't flunk," Joshua said, glaring at the tiny boy. "I'm just visiting. Tomorrow my family is moving to East Africa."

By the time the final bell for school had rung and Mrs. Goodwin's class was full of the smallest people he had ever seen gathered together in the same room with him, Joshua had developed a serious stomachache and asked to be sent to the school nurse immediately.

"After the spelling test," Mrs. Goodwin said as she passed out paper for the first spelling test of the year.

"I may be dead after the spelling test," Joshua said, but he took the test anyway, scored a 50 as usual, and asked to be excused to go to the boys' room.

The hallway of Mirch Elementary was empty. He walked diagonally across to the fourth-grade classroom and looked through the window of the door. There, right in front of him looking like the enemy on TV, was Tommy Wilhelm, and behind Tommy was Andrew Porter, Joshua's best friend from Mrs. Nice's class, the only person in the whole world that at this moment in his life he liked a bit. Including his parents.

Bravely, he opened the fourth-grade class-room door, walked up to the desk of a new teacher hired that year to teach fourth grade, and said that he had to see Andrew Porter immediately. It was an emergency.

"How come you're not in this class, Josh?" someone called from the back of the room.

"He flunked," Billy Nickel, the only seri-ously stupid boy from Mrs. Nice's third grade, said thoughtfully. "My mother told me last night."

"That's a lie," Andrew said.

"I saw him go into Mrs. Goodwin's class with his parents this morning," Tommy Wil-helm said. "I don't think he was going to a birthday party."

"Please," the new teacher said, rising from her desk. "It's time for social studies."

"I'm actually moving away," Joshua said as loud as he could, which wasn't very loud because his voice was filling with tears.

Andrew agreed that Joshua Bates was

telling the absolute truth. He knew, he said, because they were best friends. "His father told me they were moving last night on the telephone."

"Liars," Tommy Wilhelm sang out as Joshua left the classroom with Andrew Porter.

In the empty boys' room Joshua started to cry in spite of himself.

"I mean, Billy Nickel was ten times worse at reading than me," Joshua said.

"I know," Andrew agreed sympathetically. "And so were Tommy Aiken and John Starer."

"And Dickie Fluger."

"It's unfair," Andrew said sadly.

"So I'm running away. Blowing town. Beating it. Mrs. Goodwin is a tank," Joshua said, feeling his strength return.

They leaned against the windowsill. The window was half open, over the playground full of kindergarten children swinging and playing in the sandbox.

"Where'll you go?" Andrew asked.

"East Africa."

"Alone?"

"Do you want to come?" Joshua asked brightly. "We could have a really good time."

"Well," Andrew said. "Probably I can't. My parents wouldn't let me."

There was a knock on the bathroom door and Mrs. Goodwin called in her low, gravelly voice.

"Joshua? Are you all right?"

Joshua didn't answer.

"Joshua?"

"I'm not dead if that's what you mean," he replied.

"We better go," Andrew whispered. "I don't want to spend the day with the principal." He reached into his pocket and took out two plastic standing Union soldiers with rifles pointing. "You can have them," he said. "They're extras. I'll see you on the playground in an hour."

Back in the classroom Joshua told Mrs. Goodwin that he had the flu and needed to go home pronto or everybody else in the third grade would catch it.

Mrs. Goodwin put her hand on his forehead. "You're not hot," she said. "You'll last until three o'clock."

"You'll be sorry," Joshua said darkly.

"We'll see how you feel after reading," Mrs. Goodwin said. "I need you to help me in reading class."

So Joshua stayed through reading class, moving his chair next to the child in the hippopotamus dress, who needed special help with phonics.

"I won't read aloud, you know," he said to Mrs. Goodwin as she passed his desk.

"I wouldn't dream of asking you," she said.

During social studies Mrs. Goodwin asked Joshua to explain about the lives of Indians on reservations, which he did. She didn't mention the fact that Joshua knew about Indians because he had already studied them in third grade once. She simply acted as if Joshua T. Bates, formerly retarded, was the smartest boy she had met in several months.

By recess Joshua had almost forgotten his stomachache and was helping a new boy from Peru add three digits.

As he left the classroom to go to the playground, Mrs. Goodwin called to him.

"I'm sorry to hear you have to leave town tomorrow," she said.

He shrugged. "Who knows? Maybe my plans will change."

From
Fourth Grade Rats
by Jerry Spinelli

9

"First grade babies! Second grade cats! Third grade angels! Fourth grade rats!"

Suds Morton is finally in fourth grade but sometimes he wishes he could have stayed a third-grader. His friend Joey thinks being a rat is great. He says rats don't cry, and rats push the little kids off the swings. Suds may not be an angel, but he's not so sure he wants to be a rat.

Our school yard has two tire swings. The tires hang on ropes from a bar. You just plunk your rear end on a tire and swing. Or just sit, if you want.

The tires hang almost to the ground. That's so the littlest kids in school can climb onto them.

And that's the situation me and Joey walked into after school. We were going to powwow at the tire swings, but two little kids were already there. They looked like first-graders.

"Guess *they'll* have to find another place," Joey said.

He lifted one of the first-graders out of his tire, plunked him on the ground, and sat in the tire himself.

The first-grader's face got red. His ears got red. "You rat!" he yelled.

Joey nodded and smirked. "You got that right, kid."

All eyes swung to me. Would I do the same as Joey?

The kid on the other tire looked feistier than her pal. From the look in her eyes, you might have thought she was a ten-foot cat and I was a mouse.

Nobody got a chance to see what I would do, because suddenly the kid bolted. Tore out of there and left the tire swaying on the rope. I realized she may have looked feisty, but she was scared.

The other kid took off, too. But not before he yelled, "Rat!" and spit at me. Missed by a mile. First-graders are not good spitters.

"Sit down," said Joey.

I sat on the tire. "I don't feel right about that," I said.

"About what?"

"About kicking those little kids out."

I kept seeing the girl's eyes as she ran. It was the first time anyone had ever been afraid of me. I couldn't figure out how I felt about it.

"Suds," Joey said, "remember a couple summers ago? Fourth of July? At the park?"

"What about it?" I said.

"The talent show?"

"Yeah."

"The bench?"

"Huh?"

Joey got off his tire. He stood in front of me. "The *bench* we were sitting on to watch the talent show? That we didn't sit on for very long?"

"Oh, yeah . . ." It was coming back to me. "Some kids kicked us off it."

"Fourth-graders," he said. "They *dumped* us off. They lifted one end of the bench — real high — so you and me slid off, onto the ground."

I laughed, picturing Joey and me zooming down the bench like it was a sliding board. "Man, I forgot all about that."

"I didn't," said Joey. He wasn't laughing.

"So," I said, "now that I'm a fourth-grade rat, I'm supposed to go around dumping little kids off benches. Is that it?"

"There's more to it than that," he said.

I started swinging. "I'm all ears."

Joey got back on his tire. He matched his swinging to mine.

"Suds," he said, "you're in fourth grade now. That makes you a rat. Stop fighting it. It's nature's way."

"I can fight it if I want."

"Yeah? How?"

I thought for a minute. "I'll do rotten in school. I'll do so rotten, they'll have to flunk me back to third grade."

"Forget it, dude. You can't go backwards. Time marches on."

"I *liked* being an angel."

Joey stopped his swing. He reached over and stopped mine. "Suds, you ant brain. Angels finish last. What did you ever get out of it, huh? Did anybody ever say, 'Oh, thank you, Suds. You're so nice. You're such an angel.' Huh? Anybody ever say that?"

"Not exactly," I had to admit.

"Your mother ever say, 'Oh, Suds, you're such an angel, you don't have to clean your room anymore'?"

"Guess not."

"Are you allowed to stay up late?"

"No."

"Are you allowed to go anywhere you want by yourself?"

"No."

"Are you allowed to say no to your mom?"

" 'Course not."

He poked my tire. "See. That's what I'm talking about."

"I'm glad *you* know what you're talking about," I said, "because *I* sure don't."

"I'm talking about growing up," he said. "I'm talking about not being an angel baby anymore. I'm talking about taking care of Number One for a change."

I felt stupid, but I had to ask. "Who's this Number One?"

He pointed. "You, dude. You're Number One, for you. I'm Number One for me."

Number One. That sounded good. Maybe there was something to this rat business, after all.

"But what about crying?" I said. "Why can't I cry or be scared of spiders?"

He got off his tire. He faced me. He was dead serious. "Because real men don't cry."

"What's men got to do with it? Before, you said it's rats that don't cry."

"That's right," he said. "That's the whole point. Being a rat is the next step up to being a man. You want to be a man, don't you?"

"Sure," I said. "I guess so."

"Well," he said, "you can't be a man without being a rat first." He poked me in the chest. "That's what fourth grade is all about."

Except for us, the school yard was empty. Parents were calling their kids in to dinner.

We headed home. As I walked up the driveway to my house, Joey said, "See ya, rat."

"See ya," I said.

Before I reached the door, he rushed back. He grabbed my arm. "Don't forget," he whispered. "Say no to your mom."